MW01504767

The Freudian Slip Murder

ALSO BY JEANNE QUIGLEY

Veronica Walsh Mysteries

All Things Murder

Murder, by George

Cast for Murder

The Freudian Slip Murder

Robyn Cavanagh Mysteries

The Double Exposure Murder

The Freudian Slip Murder

A Veronica Walsh Mystery

JEANNE QUIGLEY

Copyright © 2023 by Jeanne Quigley

This novel is a work of fiction. Names, characters, places, and incidents are either the product of the author's imagination, or, if real, used fictitiously.

No part of this work may be reproduced, transmitted, stored, or used in any form or by any means graphic, electronic, or mechanical means, including photocopying, recording, or by any information storage and retrieval system, without the express permission of the author or publisher, except where permitted by law.

Cover graphics from Pixabay, courtesy of Pencil Parker (cola bottle image) and 6847478 (poison bottle image).

Acknowledgements

I'm grateful to Veronica Walsh fans who 've stayed with the series through the long delay. Thank you for your patience and the warm embrace you've given Veronica and me. Your support means the world to me.

To my niece Shannon Fegan, thank you for the helpful tips you shared on the cover design. You reminded me that less is more.

Thank you to my friend Charles Fortier for your thorough reading of the manuscript, kindhearted exposure of my goofs, and excellent advice. I appreciate them all.

My thanks to Nancy Moskowitz of the New City Library for her constant encouragement of my writing and enthusiasm for the Veronica Walsh series. You're wonderful, Nancy!

I'm indebted to cozy mystery bloggers Lori Caswell, Yvonne Hering, Kathy Kaminski, and Dru Ann Love for helping me introduce the Veronica Walsh series almost ten years ago. Your support made all the difference and I am forever grateful to each of you.

Professor Robert Slabey, you inspired this book's title way back in 1987. Your delightful wit has not been forgotten. Thank you. May you rest in peace.

For my cousin Eileen Habacker. My childhood pen pal, first beta reader, lifelong friend. Thank you, Eileen, for always cheering me on in all things.

Chapter One

"What's under every academic gown?"

I tore a small piece from my sandwich's pumpernickel bread and tossed the morsel to a blue jay foraging in the grass several feet from the bench where my best friend and I sat.

"Hmm..." Carol made a show of considering my question. "A black cashmere turtleneck and a tweed jacket with elbow patches and a pipe in the chest pocket. And wool pants and penny loafers."

"A stereotypical but educated guess." I allowed myself a dramatic pause. "But wrong. Under every academic gown is a Freudian slip."

Carol groaned and slid her sunglasses a couple of centimeters down the bridge of her nose. The better to give me an amused flash of her brown eyes. "Where did you hear that joke? Did Mark bring it home from a recent faculty meeting?" She picked up the paper cup standing on the bench between us and took a sip of her soda.

"An English professor told it in a class I took my sophomore year. Twentieth-Century American Fiction. Professor Slabey. A very entertaining man."

"He must have been for you to remember a joke he told decades ago."

"It seems like only yesterday."

We laughed and settled into a short silence. I took a bite from my turkey sandwich and surveyed Barton's tranquil park.

It was a splendid day in the first week of May. Though spring had officially arrived six weeks earlier and many of its blooms—daffodils, crocuses, forsythia, and dogwood among them—had already come and gone, I still savored each bright new day in Barton. My hometown, a dozen square miles of charm and beauty in the Adirondack region of upstate New York, had withstood a winter defined by record-setting low temperatures and a high accumulation of snow.

Carol and I often had breakfast or lunch together. During the long winter months, we'd eaten inside at the bakery or deli, at Carol's flower shop, or in my small office at All Things, the boutique I'd purchased the previous summer. It was a pleasure to share our meals outdoors again, whether seated on a bench along Orchard Street or in the park.

"What made you think of the joke?" Carol dipped her hand into the family-size bag of potato chips I'd brought to share.

"Mark and I are going to a barbecue at his colleague's home on Saturday." Mark Burke, a lifelong friend who had become my "significant other" around the same time I bought All Things, was a history professor at nearby Arden College. "Susanna's husband is a psychology professor, and they're both the heads of their departments."

"Imagine their dinner conversation," Carol said. "Though they surely also argue over who takes out the garbage and does the dishes. I'm sure they'll love your joke."

"I think the psychologists in the group will particularly appreciate it. There will probably be a Freudian or two among them."

"I hope they're polite and don't ruin the punch line." Carol popped the last bit of her sandwich into her mouth and wiped her fingers on a paper napkin.

I swallowed the last mouthful of my ginger ale and grabbed the chip bag. Carol tossed our empty cups and sandwich wrappers in the trash and we ambled through the park to its Orchard Street entrance.

"I bet the psychology professors will be curious about your

soap career. All those bedroom scenes..." Carol's voice trailed off into a snicker.

"That would be a feast for psychoanalysis."

I entertained a few memories from my three-decade acting career, which I'd spent portraying the character Rachel Wesley on the soap opera *Days and Nights*. The soap plots were loaded with drama and trauma that would keep real-life psychologists and psychiatrists busy forever.

"I might end up on a chaise lounge with ten psychology professors surrounding me, notepads in hand, asking me how playing a married-multiple-times character affected my real love life." I came to a sudden halt in front of the dry cleaner. "Good grief, I've never thought of that. Maybe I'm a fifty-something, never-married woman because my soap character's marital failures made me a commitment-phobe. And I never realized it because it's buried deep in my subconscious!"

Carol put her hand on my shoulder and, her voice gentle yet firm, said, "Don't be a drama queen."

I exhaled my sudden panic. "You're right. Thanks, pal."

We continued along Orchard Street, Barton's version of Main Street U.S.A. Both sides of Orchard were dotted with linden trees and various annual flowers planted in large wooden barrels. The natural beauties, along with the charming facades of the shops—all of which were owned by residents of Barton and not corporations headquartered in far-off cities—made Barton one of the top-twenty prettiest towns in New York state and an attraction to tourists throughout the year.

Carol broke our silence when we neared All Things. "I wonder if a Jungian heart beats under the Freudian slip."

"If I add that to the joke I'll spark a lively debate between the Freudians and Jungians," I said, laughing.

Carol chortled, "And expose the big egos on campus."

"Including well-developed super egos. How about this. An id, an ego, and a super ego walk into a bar ..."

Our fit of giggles, more suitable for current co-eds than two women several years beyond middle-age, propelled us to my shop's door.

"I think what the professors will be most interested in is how you pieced together evidence to solve three murders."

"I hope not. That might be *parlor talk* for the academic crowd, but it's a party pooper for me."

We wished each other a good afternoon and Carol continued up Orchard to her shop on the next block. I lingered outside All Things for a minute, soaking up the sunshine and refreshing breeze. Traffic—pedestrian and automobile—was light along Orchard, with residents and visitors alike moving through the day at leisure. After decades of working in Manhattan and dealing with the city's frantic pace, I appreciated the gentle movements of Barton.

I gave a final thought to the barbecue and my joke. Maybe I would add Carol's second punchline, elicit a hearty chuckle, and impress the intellectuals with my wit and charm.

"Ha!" I said aloud. "I'll either be the hit of the party, or I'll never be invited back."

Chapter Two

I'd accompanied Mark to Derek Morley and Susanna Rafferty's home once before, a few months earlier for a dinner party. They lived in a Colonial-style home on a street shaded by sycamores and maples. Each house had a wide swath of grass for a front yard and a mailbox set at the end of the driveway to spare the mail deliver the perilous journey across a snow-and-ice-covered lawn and driveway in the winter.

We walked around to the back of the house, where a staircase of more than a dozen steps led up to a deck that stretched the width of the house and overlooked a secluded yard. Though we weren't fashionably late, the party was already in full swing.

Our hostess greeted us at the top of the stairs. Susanna, a slim woman who was about my age, welcomed us. "How lovely!" she said of the bouquet I handed her. Delight lit her cocoa-brown eyes and she lifted the flowers to her nose for a sample of their delicate fragrance.

Derek, holding a martini glass filled with his favored Sidecar cocktail, joined us. "It's good to see you again, Veronica." He leaned in and brushed my cheek with a kiss. The whiskers of his gray-streaked goatee tickled my skin.

He offered his hand to Mark. "Congratulations on another year in the books. I assume your Van Buren biography is still on course for a fall release?"

"It is," Mark said.

Derek and Mark talked for a minute about the biography Mark had written of Martin Van Buren, the nineteenth-century president and short-time New York governor. "I look forward to reading the book. Susanna says it's excellent. But right now you need refreshments." Derek gestured for us to accompany him to the bar, which was set up on the far side of the deck on a folding table covered with a blue-and-white plaid tablecloth.

We were joined by two women and a man. Derek introduced me to the trio: Miranda Liu and Bradley Robbins, both members of the psychology faculty, and the department's administrative assistant, Noelle Lopez.

Miranda raised her glass in salute. "This isn't only our celebration of the end of an academic year. Veronica, you'll soon be celebrating your first anniversary as proprietor of All Things. Cheers to you."

"Thanks. And I include the boutique's staff in that toast. Without their knowledge and experience, the shop would've closed within a month with me in charge."

"You're wrong about that, Veronica," Miranda countered. "There was that article in the newspaper a couple of months ago on how all of Barton's shops have seen an increase in business since you took over All Things. Your fans miss seeing you on television every day. So they flock to the village to support your boutique and then patronize many of the other wonderful shops."

"They come to see you and leave having supported the entire Barton creative community." Noelle offered me a warm smile, her dark eyes conveying gracious respect. "Your stature and leadership of the boutique has elevated the profile of many of our local artists. I know one artist—Lisette Rosen—who received an order for a full set of glassware from a Pennsylvania woman after she bought one of Lisette's vases at your shop. And Lisette told me that a local carpenter got a commission for a dining room table from a New Jersey couple *and* a ceramicist who's sold four of her creations via her website to a woman who *discovered* her at your shop. I'm sure they're not the only artists who've gained a following thanks to you.

Your fanbase has expanding the fanbases of our artists. Well done."

Noelle's compliment added a few extra beats to my heart. I humbly basked in the praise. "I'm proud that my little shop on the corner of Orchard and Sycamore contributes to everyone's success. I enjoy being a supporting player to our talented residents."

"I wouldn't be surprised if you win Businesswoman of the Year," Miranda said. She swept aside the stray lock of her angle-cut black hair that brushed her cheek.

"I wouldn't go that far," I said. "What would I do for an encore?"

The group gave a collective chuckle and I, not for the first time, gave myself a mental pat on the back for taking the risk, and having the wisdom, to buy All Things.

The spotlight shifted to a boy who dashed into the yard from the neighbor's property. The blond-headed tyke, who looked to be about six, chased after a soccer ball. Behind him ran a smaller boy, also fair-haired.

"I got it!" the older boy yelled. The ball rolled half-way across the lawn before he reached it.

"That's Tyler and Caleb," Susanna said. "Hi, boys!"

I noted the sweetness in her voice and the sourness in Derek's expression.

"They have two-year-old twin sisters. And here they are! Hello, Josie and Eliza." Susanna stepped over to the deck rail and waved at the two toddlers who had joined the party.

Both girls had their golden-blonde hair pulled up into pigtails and wore blue jeans and matching pink T-shirts with white heart decals across the chest. One of the girls changed course and charged over to and up the deck stairs.

"Party crasher," Miranda said, laughing.

"Undisciplined children." Derek's eyes narrowed as the girl neared.

"Mine!" The girl blazed a path to a short table set between two deck chairs. On the table was a plate of cheese and crackers. She did a double-fisted snack grab before Susanna could remove the plate from the tot's reach. The girl shoved a cracker into her mouth.

Susanna held the girl's other hand to prevent her from eating the second cracker before she had swallowed the first. "Josie, chew."

Josie rolled her eyes and made a show of chomping her jaw.

The kids' parents had appeared and were corralling the boys and Josie's twin amid the boys' back-and-forth toss of the ball and Eliza's tears and cries of "Me eat too!"

The mother jogged up the deck stairs. Josie spotted her and darted to the beverage table.

"She wants to wash down the crackers with a cocktail," Bradley quipped.

"Oh, no you don't." Derek blocked Josie by putting his hand on her head.

The girl made a fist, shook it at Derek, and punched his calf.

Derek leaned over the girl. "I'm going to call the police on you."

The girl slapped Derek's head and attempted to grasp his close-cut black hair.

Derek laughed and straightened. "Thwarted!"

"Josie!" her mother scolded. "Sorry." Her gaze shifted from Derek to Susanna to include both in her apology.

Josie ran across the deck and was grabbed by her mother before she reached the stairs.

"Disaster averted," I whispered to Miranda.

"It's fine, Vicki," Susanna said in an assuring tone. "We love when our young neighbors visit."

Vicki scooped up Josie and kissed the child's forehead. "We didn't mean to crash your party. Say bye-bye."

Josie didn't bid adieu. She gave a longing glance to the plate still in Susanna's hands and stretched her arm toward the plate. "More!"

"We have snacks at home." Vicki adjusted her hold on the girl and trotted down the stairs.

Her husband, who had his fingers encircled around Eliza's wrist, gave us a wave of apology.

"So those are the neighbors." Bradley threw a humored glance at Derek.

"Vicki fancies herself a psychologist," Derek said. "She has a channel on one of those video-sharing websites with clips of her children participating in her various *studies*. Her word, not mine."

"What kind of studies?" I asked.

"Her latest is some challenge that many parents are conducting and sharing with the world. Vicki will place a treat—often candy—in front of the children and tell them not to touch it until she returns. She'll leave the room for a minute. When she comes back, she makes a big show of praising the children who obeyed and scolding those who haven't. It's all for the audience. Performative parenting." Derek sneered and sipped his cocktail. "She's called me over there several times to watch her latest video and solicits my professional opinion. Yesterday afternoon, most recently."

"Did you call her a self-absorbed mommy? Her children spoiled brats? I can picture you lambasting her parenting skills." Miranda's smirk indicated her amusement over Derek's predicament.

"I told Vicki to stop using her children to secure the attention her insecure ego needs," Derek said. "I suggested she put her cell phone down and *parent* her children or they'll need a professional psychologist within five years. Setting a bowl of candy in front of your children, telling them not to eat any, and leaving the room isn't the way to instill in them patience and self-control." He waved his hand at the cheese and cracker plate Susanna had returned to the side table. "From the children's scarfing of our food, it's obvious Vicki has a lot of work to do."

"Everyone's a psychologist these days." Bradley's lighthearted remark took the sharpness out of Derek's diatribe.

"I shouldn't let it bother me." Derek sipped his drink. "Social media is your area of expertise, Bradley. I should introduce you to Vicki. You can do a study on *her*. Title it *Parenting in the Twenty-first Century*. How parents today have a much wider audience for their *home movies* of their kids. Just whip out their phone, film the kid, and post it online. Dangerous stuff."

We all murmured agreement of Derek's observation.

"Vicki would be the more interesting subject." Miranda's gaze lingered on the path the family had trod back to their house. "We should go over there and steal her snacks. See how she reacts."

Susanna clicked her tongue and said in earnest, "Let's not savage the neighbors over our cocktails. The Shepards are a lovely family."

"They are." Derek's agreement came with a facetious twist. "And though I won't *officially* study them, I will be observing them from afar."

Mark said, "From your deck, with a drink in your hand."

Derek laughed at Mark's gentle tease. "A bit of alcohol will certainly make my observation more enjoyable. I admit, I'm interested in who those four children will be in fifteen years. I have a theory—"

Susanna tugged on her husband's arm. "None of your theories today, darling. No shop talk. You are not addressing a conference of psychologists or at work in your lab."

Derek put his arm around her and his amber eyes brightened. "A thousand apologies, my dear." He kissed her cheek. "But am I allowed to talk with Mark about his Van Buren book?"

"You're always allowed to engage in my *shop's* talk."

Our group broke up and Miranda took my arm and guided me to the deck rail. "I'd love to talk more about your acting career and your transition into a businesswoman. Do you think we can get together sometime for a casual interview? Over lunch, perhaps?"

"Sure. I always like to talk about the good old days. And about myself."

Miranda's laughter rose above the party chatter. "I'll call you."

A while later I went into the house to visit the bathroom. I stepped into a kitchen of black granite counters, stainless steel appliances, and an island large enough that the guests could gather around if a sudden storm forced the party inside. I continued down the hall that connected the kitchen to the front of the house. In the entrance foyer I turned right and came within inches of bumping into Bradley.

"Excuse me, Veronica." He stepped back, his startled expression fading. "I heard Miranda book you for an interview."

"More of a conversation over lunch."

"I hope you don't have a limit on how many *conversations* you have," Bradley said, his grin coy.

"Requests for interviews dropped precipitously after my soap was canceled," I said. "So I'm grateful to anyone who's still interested in my career. I assume that's what you'd like to talk about?"

"Yes, but from a different perspective."

"What would that perspective be?" I asked, my glance resting for a brief moment on the soft waves of his dark-blonde hair. *I bet his students daydream of running their fingers through those silken locks.*

Bradley struck a conversational pose, with his left arm across his chest and his right elbow resting on his wrist. With a flourish of his hand, he explained his proposal. "I've done much research on teenagers' gossip and what effects it has on their lives. I'd like to study the significance of gossip among adults and the impact it has on personal and professional lives."

I had been the subject of several gossip stories over my acting career. The majority of the stories contained innocuous rumors about my dating a co-star, though a few tales that made out that I had a bitter real-life rivalry with the actress who played my soap character's arch-enemy were terrible lies.

"I have some experience with the gossip grapevine. Derek mentioned that social media is your area of interest," I said. "That has contributed greatly to the problem."

He gave a solemn nod. "It has destroyed many young people. I won't go into the statistics. I'm sure you've heard the stories that have made national news. The grapevine has grown deadly shoots."

"For most of my career, all I had to contend with was soap magazines. When the Internet came along, most of the gossip was focused on the younger generation of soap actors."

"I'd appreciate hearing about your experiences," Bradley said. "May I call you in a few days to schedule a meeting?"

I agreed, gave him my cell number, and we parted. I turned right, passed the staircase to the second floor. Before stepping into the bathroom, I stole a glance at the open doorway at the end of the hall, attracted by a framed print on the wall opposite the door. It featured a dark-haired man in a suit looking into a mirror were visible from where I stood. The curiosity of the painting was that the man's reflection wasn't of his face, but of his back.

"Interesting," I murmured.

I emerged a couple of minutes later and met Derek in the hall from the kitchen. He held a silver cocktail shaker. "How does our gathering of academics compare to your actor soirées of years past? We surely match the many post-Emmy parties you've attended?"

"Of course. Even better, because at this party, everyone's a winner. We told each other that at Emmy parties, but no one believed it."

Derek chuckled and gestured for me to accompany him into the living room. "I would've loved to have been a fly on that wall. Winners and runners-up and those who didn't even make the nominees' list. It would've been rich ground for observation." He crossed the room to a cabinet in the corner. He opened it and withdrew a bottle of cognac with a familiar gold label, the brand name and "XO" written in bold red lettering. The "XO" meant the cognac was extra old, or had been aged for at least ten years.

Didn't want to put out your hundred-dollar booze out for the guests, huh?

"You wouldn't have observed much," I said, standing up for my fellow soap actors. "We just all had a great time catching up with friends we hadn't seen in a while."

I ignored the familiar jab of melancholy I still sometimes had for my former career and admired the room's elegant contents while he filled his glass. It was furnished with a set of mission-style chairs and a couch and love seat pair covered in a rich cream-colored fabric. On a table placed by the front window were a few framed photos of Derek and Susanna. On the wall to the right of the window hung a print of Gilbert Stuart's portrait of George Washington and on the narrow adjacent wall was a portrait of Martha Washington. On the wall on the other side of the wide entry from the front hall was a painting of Washington and Betsy Ross, the first American flag draped on her lap. An area rug with a lattice design in shades of ivory and sage green covered a section of the gleaming mahogany floors.

I went over to the fireplace where busts of Washington, Sigmund Freud, and Abraham Lincoln surveyed the room from the marble mantel. "What do you think Freud would say of Washington and Lincoln?"

Derek, holding the cognac bottle to his chest, moved to stand beside me. "Sigmund would be fascinated by their egos. Washington, you know, had a huge ego when he was a young man. Got it under control and became a great leader."

"So the title *Father of Our Country* wouldn't give him a case of the *big head*?"

"He bore the designation with humility."

I thought it a good time for my well-practiced quip. "I have a question. What's under every academic gown?"

He tilted his head to one side, his eyes glinting with amusement. "A Freudian slip!"

"You must have heard that a thousand times."

"Yes, but only from stuffy academics. Never by an actress who has an Emmy trophy on her mantel."

"I keep my Emmy in the china cabinet. Your display has me considering getting a bust of Irna Phillips and placing it on my mantel. She created the first daytime soap way back in the forties. We call her the *Queen of Soaps*."

Derek laughed. "You have a delightful sense of humor, Veronica. Do you know what's under the Freudian slip?"

"No! And I want to know. Something Jungian? Or maybe Piaget or Skinner?"

Derek shook his head. "I don't know. We'll have to plumb the depths of our subsciouses to come up with an answer." He chuckled. "Do you watch any of the soap operas still on television?"

"I sneak a peek once in a while."

"And what do you think of what you see? What is your opinion on the current state of the soap opera?"

Derek's curiosity surprised me. *Does he really care about soaps? Is he working on some project too and he wants me to participate? Or maybe he's simply a good host showing interest in a guest.*

I chose diplomacy over a full review of what I thought about the storylines and quality of acting on the quartet of soaps still on the air. "I'm glad four are still on network T.V. There's still an audience, though much smaller than it was in our heyday."

"Yes, of course. That's due, in part, to more women working outside the home and the hundreds more channels cable television has given us to watch. But what do you think of the soaps? The storylines and characters? The quality? Are they wisely using the thirty or sixty minutes they've been given?" Derek asked. "I don't watch soaps, never have, but I took some time yesterday and did a bit of research on current soap plots. Nothing of substance. Just nonsense, unrealistic storylines that speak nothing to the social issues of today."

I wanted to correct him and defend my *home team*, but I wasn't a regular viewer and couldn't back up my argument with current storylines. The last time I'd caught a few minutes of a soap, the day's episode featured the lead male character agonizing over the decision of which woman he wanted to marry: the mother of his first-born child or the mother of his second child. A month separated the children's births. I'd turned the television off after a few minutes, my mood gloomy by the inanity of the storyline.

"Soaps have gotten a bit absurd," I conceded. "What about the state of your profession? What's your opinion on the folks who *practice*," I made air quotes, "psychology on television and social media?"

Derek's grin turned wry. "There are no Freuds, Jungs, or Piagets among them, I'm afraid. Everyone has an observation today on human behavior that they think is unique." Derek raised the cocktail shaker, creating a tinkling sound from the ice cubes within the container. "Social media panders to those with short attention spans. People don't *read* articles they find online, they *scan* them. They don't want to listen to a one-hour lecture. They need the information given to them in three minutes. And yet so many have become *stars* thanks to this medium."

He returned to the liquor cabinet, poured a measure of cognac into the cocktail shaker, and put the bottle in the cabinet. He withdrew a bottle of orange liqueur, poured a measure of that into the shot glass, and tipped the shot glass into the shaker.

"It demeans the study and scholarship of the field," he continued. "Even colleagues and contemporaries are wading into the shallow end of the research pool."

"And your students? Do they give you hope for the future of your profession?"

His frown quirked into a wry grin. "Some do, yes. Some I have to encourage to explore the deep end of that pool. Others are stuck on their view of the world and don't want to swim at all."

After returning the liqueur to the cabinet, Derek led me through the dining room and into the kitchen, where he gave the shaker a vigorous jiggle over the sink and poured the fresh drink into his martini glass.

Derek then moved to the slider. "Enjoy your lunch with Miranda." He winked, opened the screen door, and moved aside for me to step through to the deck.

I didn't ask in which end of the "research pool" he thought Miranda swam. By his wink and tone, I had a fair idea.

Chapter Three

"What are your plans for the day?"

Mark took a drink of his black coffee. "Start writing the speech I'm giving at that conference in Syracuse next month. And I'm going to go over to campus to start reading the materials for an external review I agreed to give."

"What's an external review?" I took a bite from my cheese danish and glanced out the window to Orchard Street. Mark and I sat at a table at Rizzuto's bakery and enjoyed breakfast before we started our Tuesday workday.

"It's a part of the tenure process. When a person is up for a tenured position, several professors—five or six, usually—from peer institutions whose expertise is in the candidate's area are asked to review the candidate's work. Research papers, published writing, etcetera, and give an opinion on whether the person would be offered tenure at their university."

"That's interesting. How many times have you been asked to do a review?"

"A few times. I've declined a couple of invitations due to other commitments. This is the third review I've agreed to do." At the ring of his cell, Mark took his phone from his jeans pocket and answered the call.

I took the last sips of my coffee and bites of my danish and half-listened to Mark's conversation.

"That's awful. Was Susanna with him?" Mark listened for about thirty seconds, his somber gaze fixed on the table. "I'm sorry to hear this. I was going to come by campus this morning. I'll be there in about half an hour."

Mark ended the call and set the phone on the table. "Derek passed away last night."

"What? What happened?" My thoughts went to the barbecue and Derek's obvious vigor, both physical and intellectual. He looked fit and sounded strong.

"He had a heart attack, apparently. Susanna had an evening meeting on campus. When she left the house, Derek was having a cocktail on the deck. When she returned a couple of hours later, she found him at the bottom of the deck stairs."

"Oh, how terrible!" I fought to erase the sudden image of Derek tumbling down the long flight of steps from the deck to the hard slate on the ground.

"He'd vomited on the deck. Susanna thinks he got up to go inside to the bathroom, got dizzy and disoriented, and fell down the stairs."

In my mind's eye a vision of Susanna discovering her husband dead outside their house replaced the picture of Derek's fall. I clicked my tongue in sympathy for the new widow's nightmare. "Poor Susanna. She must be devastated."

Mark nodded. "They were going to celebrate their twenty-seventh anniversary in August."

"Did Derek have a heart problem?"

Mark finished his coffee. "Not that I know of. He'd never mentioned any health issue and Susanna has never said anything."

We lingered at the table for another minute until our shock over the news faded. On the sidewalk outside the bakery I said, "I'll go to Carol's this morning and have an arrangement sent to Susanna."

"Thanks, love."

We exchanged a goodbye kiss and then Mark embraced me. I leaned into the hug, pressing my cheek against his chest and inhaling the scent of his cologne. I thought of Susanna and Derek's anniversary; Mark and I would soon mark one year in our sweet relationship. It was a late bloom, but I hoped we still had a few decades to go together. Derek's death was a frightening reality check.

The tenderness reflected in Mark's eyes told me he had the same thought. "I'll call you later." He dug into his pocket for his car keys.

"If you talk with Susanna, give her my sympathies."

We parted after a second kiss. "Drive carefully," I called to Mark before turning and heading to the end of the block and All Things, my shop on the corner.

I took a mid-morning break and headed up Orchard to Emerson Florist. I'm a frequent visitor to the shop, not only to see my best friend, but also to spend time among the fragrant and gorgeous inventory Carol maintains. Floral therapy, I call it.

Carol stood behind the counter, studying something on her tablet. She registered surprise at my entrance. "It's too late for breakfast, too early for lunch, and we usually don't *do* coffee breaks. What's up?"

"I need to send a condolence bouquet. Derek Morley, the host of the barbecue Mark and I went to on Saturday, passed away last evening. His wife, Susanna, thinks he had a heart attack."

"Oh, how sad. Was she with him?"

"No." I repeated what Mark had told me of how Susanna had found her husband.

"Poor woman." Carol walked from behind the counter. "I'll keep them both in my prayers. Do you have anything in particular in mind for the bouquet?"

Carol and I spent the next few minutes selecting flowers for the arrangement. I chose soft shades of pink, lavender, and white for an array I hoped would console Susanna.

I followed Carol to her backroom workshop and watched her arrange the flowers in a large vase.

"How old was Derek?" she asked, cutting the stems of the flowers with an adept wielding of a floral knife.

"He was about our age. Maybe a year or two older."

"That gives me a chill." Carol lowered the knife and gave me a look. "We're not getting any younger."

"I know. It's scary. Susanna never mentioned that Derek had a heart problem."

"Maybe he didn't know he had one."

"Maybe. I need to start eating healthier and exercising more."

"You get a lot of exercise." Carol was making beautiful progress in creating the bouquet. "You walk to work almost every day and you come up here all the time. I rarely walk down to All Things."

"It's easier for me to get away from the shop."

"Yeah. Plus you're up and down the stairs to your office how many times a day? That's great weight-bearing exercise. Good for the bones."

"You do a lot of weightlifting too. Toting those buckets of flowers and the arrangements around the shop. And you have floral therapy all day long. Isn't working with flowers calming? Your blood pressure must be perfect."

Carol grinned at our rationalizations. "The florist version of owning a dog or cat? Instead of reducing stress by petting an animal, I'm doing it by plopping roses in a vase?"

"Yep." We shared a laugh. "Think of how much less stress everyone on a plane would feel if travelers were given small bouquets when they boarded? The delightful floral scent would calm their nerves. They'd be soothed just by looking at the flowers."

"I think you just discovered world peace."

We had another laugh before falling into a short silence. "Nothing makes you reflect on your life more than someone else's death," Carol said.

"So true. Maybe we should start walking around the block after we eat. And I'll start bringing something healthier than chips. Carrot and celery sticks."

"Sounds good."

Carol finished the arrangement, and we went out to the counter.

Carol rang up the order and handed me a small white card and envelope; I jotted a couple of sentences conveying sympathy, signed Mark's name and mine, and slid the card into the envelope.

"Thanks," I gave Carol Susanna's address.

"We'll deliver it once Amy or Casey returns." Carol gave me a hug. "At least you know that it's not..."

"Yeah."

I filled in Carol's ellipsis on the short walk back to All Things. "At least this isn't a murder this time."

In the year since I'd moved back to Barton, not only had I bought All Things and started a romance with Mark, I had also become the village's amateur sleuth.

My sleuthing began the morning after my arrival home. I hadn't been in Barton twenty-four hours when I found my next-door neighbor dead on her kitchen floor. Foul play was obvious—Anna's cast-iron skillet lay on the floor near her body—and I feared two friends were involved in Anna's murder. So I conducted my own investigation and ended up solving the murder. In the following months, I identified the killers of two acquaintances. My ego wasn't so big I thought the Barton police department couldn't solve the crimes without my assistance. I had a knack for sleuthing, I suppose, and for one reason or another, kept being pulled into the cases.

Derek wouldn't be another murder case to solve, however. He had died of natural causes, and my only role would be mourner at his funeral.

Chapter Four

Mark and I attended Derek's memorial service on Friday evening. The service was held on Arden's campus in the library's auditorium. A crowd of more than one hundred filled the room. I sat with Mark and two of his colleagues a few rows behind where Miranda and several others sat in the front row.

Several floral arrangements stood along the stage's apron, and on an easel placed to the right of the podium was a large photo of Derek, which I guessed was his most recent faculty photo. Four folding chairs set in a loose semi-circle had been arranged to the left of the podium.

I glanced over the service's program while murmured conversations went on around me. A quartet from Arden's music faculty would play several selections of chamber music. The college's president would be the service's first speaker, followed by Miranda, Bradley, another colleague from the psychology department, and a friend with whom Derek attended college. Susanna would be the final speaker.

Two women and two men appeared from the stage right wing and took their places on the folding chairs. The two violinists, cellist, and violist settled into their playing poses and called the assembled to silence with the opening notes of Tchaikovsky's "Andante Cantabile."

Susanna, accompanied by the eulogists, moved down the center aisle and took their places in the front row. Susanna wore a black pantsuit and light blue blouse, with her shoulder-length, golden-auburn hair held in place with a sliver clip fastened at the nape of her neck.

When the quartet finished, the president spoke for a few minutes.

Miranda then rose from her seat and ascended to the podium. She too wore a pantsuit—dark gray over a black blouse—and a somber expression that turned warm when she greeted the group.

"Thank you all for coming to this celebration of Derek Morley's life and work. I'm Miranda Liu. For those of you who don't know me, I was Derek's colleague in the psychology department for more than a decade. Derek mentored me when I joined the faculty and made the tenure process an almost pleasant endeavor." She waited for the burst of knowing laughter that filled the room subsided and then continued. "I'll always be grateful to him for the guidance he gave me in my early years and his strong advocacy of my work."

She paused for a beat. "Derek had the brilliant mind of a psychologist and the soul of a philosopher. We all know Derek loved a vigorous debate. Verbal tussles with Derek made me a better psychologist, a better teacher, and an extremely patient woman." More laughter.

Miranda talked for several minutes about her friendship with Derek and Susanna and of Derek's career achievements. Bradley then spoke of how invaluable Derek's mentorship was and of his sadness over "this sudden end to our maturing relationship."

The service went on for forty minutes of eulogies and musical interludes before Susanna closed with the most personal tribute to Derek. She thanked the speakers and the attendees, mentioned the thoughtful notes and flowers she'd received from many of Derek's counterparts at other universities, and the messages from his current and former students about the lasting impact Derek would have on their lives and careers.

She talked of their long marriage, Derek's steady companionship, and his unwavering support of her career. It was sweet and heartfelt, but Susanna did include a few quips.

"If you people thought you had it tough dealing with Derek's penchant to challenge and debate during meetings, remember I had to live with the man!" She joined the crowd's laughter. "Our relationship started with a debate that continued until the day Derek passed. Who had the greatest mind—Carl Jung or Thomas Jefferson? Who was a better father—George Washington or Sigmund Freud?" She made air quotes around *father*. "Who would win an arm-wrestling challenge—Abraham Lincoln or B.F. Skinner? I was always a staunch advocate for my guys, George, Thomas, and Abe. But today, and only today, I'll say this: Derek, you were right. Freud would beat Teddy Roosevelt in an arm-wrestling match." She paused until the laughter subsided. "As if."

At the service's end the group gathered for refreshments of coffee, tea, and cookies in the library's airy entrance foyer. I paid a visit to the ladies' room and, when I entered the high-ceilinged hall, paused at the side of the refreshment table and searched the crowd for Mark.

A man and woman in their mid-twenties stood by the coffee urn set at the center of the table. The man filled porcelain cups for his companion and himself.

The woman, who wore her reddish-brown hair in a low ponytail, looked over the crowd with a bored expression. "I just want to leave. Do you really need to have coffee? We've done our duty and made our appearance."

"Come on, Ashley. Ten more minutes. It's the right thing to do. You don't have to drink it. Just hold the cup."

"All right. For you. Not that Susanna will even notice how long you've stayed."

The dark-haired young man chided her. "I'm not doing it to impress Susanna."

"I know." Ashley gave him a peck on the cheek. "You're a sweetheart, Kyle. You honestly care about your adviser."

I spotted Mark on the other side of the hall and had taken a few steps into the crowd when Miranda approached.

I complimented her eulogy. "It was heartfelt, Miranda. I know it's difficult to lose a colleague you've worked with for many years. They become much more than a co-worker."

Miranda dipped her head in agreement. "We'll feel Derek's loss for some time." She touched my arm with a cool hand. "I hope you haven't forgotten my lunch invitation. Will you come to campus on Monday? We'll dine in the public cafeteria. It's good food, I promise."

"I haven't forgotten and I'd enjoy lunch on campus."

We set the time and parted. I weaved around several groups and neared where Mark stood with Susanna and a man I recognized from his book jacket photos and television appearances.

"Oh, Veronica, thank you for coming." Susanna, whose fair skin was makeup-free except for the dusty-rose gloss across her lips, embraced me and accepted my condolences and compliment on her eulogy. She then gestured to the man beside her. "This is my dear friend, Eric Nelson."

A medium-built, balding gentleman, Eric was a well-known presidential historian. I'd read a couple of his biographies and seen him interviewed on television several times. He'd written best-selling biographies of six presidents and had won a Pulitzer for his bio of Andrew Jackson. The go-to expert for documentaries on American history, Eric frequently appeared in public television documentaries and on Sunday morning political shows to compare and contrast the current president with previous occupants of the White House.

"Eric, this is Veronica Walsh."

The historian clasped my hand between both of his and gave it a gentle, yet firm, shake. "It's a pleasure to meet you, Veronica."

I returned the sentiment. "Though I'm sorry it is under such a sad circumstance."

Eric agreed. "I'm still in a state of disbelief over Derek's passing. He had so much passion and vitality."

"Eric and I attended Syracuse together," Susanna said. "We usually meet two or three times at conferences or when we're both on a panel. And we try to get together each summer and *not* discuss work."

The college president joined us and, after a few minutes of conversation, Mark and I excused ourselves.

Eric extended his hand to Mark. "I look forward to your Van Buren book."

The reference to Mark's upcoming biography filled me with pride. On our way to the refreshment table, I whispered, "Did you get a back-cover blurb from Eric for the book?"

"No," Mark answered.

"Line him up for your next book."

Mark gave a shy grin. "I'm glad for Susanna that so many came to honor Derek." He filled a cup with coffee and handed it to me. He filled another cup for himself.

"Including Eric Nelson." I blew across the steaming coffee and took a sip. "Do you historians have the same jealousies and rivalries that we actors have?"

"Of course we do," Mark said. "We're lucky it doesn't make the *New York Post's* Page Six or the cover of some supermarket tabloid."

"So you guys get wild with envy if someone's book sells better than yours? Or when one of you uncovers a fascinating fact about James Madison or Grover Cleveland."

"You can't tell when I'm envious." Mark's green eyes gleamed with humor. "Sure we do. We spend months doing research on an individual or historical event or period and then months putting all that information into a book we hope will be engaging and well-received. It's disappointing when a book doesn't garner attention, and if someone else succeeds with a similar book, it can be demoralizing."

"Are there ever cat fights or fist fights behind the ivy-covered walls?" I asked, teasing.

"No. We're a passive-aggressive bunch. We battle with cutting words and scathing looks."

I gave a dramatic sigh. "You people are no fun."

We drank our coffee and observed the crowd. These were Mark's *people*—he waved to several and exchanged "hellos" with a few—but

I did spot a few people I knew in the thinning crowd. Barton's police chief was there, out of uniform but still in a blue suit, and the county sheriff, also in a dark suit. They chatted with two men I didn't know.

I called Mark's attention to the foursome. "Do you know those two guys with Chief Price and the sheriff?"

"The guy to the chief's left is the head of campus security."

"I wonder—"

"There's nothing to wonder about. Are you done?" Mark took my empty coffee cup and handed it and his cup to the attendant standing behind the refreshment table. He turned me away from the huddle of law enforcers. "Shall we go?"

"Sure."

We started down the hall toward the door that led to the parking lot. I stole several glances over my shoulder at Barton's chief of police and his Arden counterpart. The chief and sheriff shook hands with the college's security boss and the unidentified man and traced our steps to the door.

Chief Price looked up from checking his phone and met my gaze. I gave him a nod of acknowledgement, turned to watch where I was walking, and slipped through the door before Mark.

Was that narrow-eyed look from the chief for me or does he have something in his eye?

I wasn't on the chief's list of favorite village residents due to my ability to solve homicide cases before his department could nab the killers, but he had no reason to give me that peeved look.

His problem, not mine.

Chapter Five

I spent Saturday morning at All Things and then, after lunch, Mark and I visited Susanna.

Susanna, dressed in jeans and a light-blue T-shirt, gave us a cheerful welcome, though the fatigue and sadness in her eyes told me the cheer was a façade. "You're going to have to help me eat these," she said of the cookies I'd picked up at Rizzuto's. "Let's sit outside."

I glanced into the living room where several vases of flowers stood on the end tables, and guessed Susanna hastened us to the deck to escape the funereal atmosphere of the house.

Odd though, that she's fleeing to the scene of her husband's death.

While Susanna was in the kitchen getting refreshments, Mark and I enjoyed the song of the birds in the wooded area beyond the yard. She returned in a couple of minutes with glasses filled with iced tea and the cookies arranged on a plate.

"Thank you for coming to the service." Susanna sat in the chair beside mine. "And for your friendship, Mark. And yours too, Veronica. You're so sweet."

I murmured words of sympathy and Mark said, "Derek will be missed. I always enjoyed spending time with him."

Susanna sipped her drink. "It's hard to think we were all gathered here a week ago. A few times I've thought, if only Derek had suffered his heart attack then, we could have saved him! Why did he have to be all alone?"

"Don't play *What If.*"

Susanna nodded at Mark's remark. "I know I shouldn't." She set her glass on the table next to her chair and leaned back. "But I can't get it out of my head. Coming home and finding Derek sprawled at the foot of the stairs." She waved her hand in a gesture of outlining Derek's prone form. "He's haunting my dreams."

Tears pooled in her eyes and she continued before Mark or I could offer a soothing word. "I feel so guilty. I should have been here to take care of my husband. And if I couldn't have saved him, at least I would have been with him in his last moment. It breaks my heart that he was alone." Susanna wiped her eyes with a paper napkin. "I can imagine Derek saying my guilt is misplaced and chiding me for trying to take responsibility for an act of nature."

"He'd be right. Don't add guilt to your grief. And why are you, a history professor, psychoanalyzing yourself?"

After we laughed over Mark's quip, I asked, "May I make a suggestion?"

"Please do!" Susanna leaned forward, eager to hear my advice.

"Getting out of the house will help. Spend time on campus. Go to lunch with a friend. Window shop on Orchard Street."

"You're right. Others have said the same to me." Susanna nodded. "I had planned a trip in early August to Massachusetts to do some research for a book I'm planning on Abigail Adams. I've thought of postponing it, but now I think I'll take it and add some leisure time to the break."

The faint jingle of the doorbell drew our attention.

"I wonder who that is?" Susanna stood and moved to the sliding door. "I'm not expecting anyone."

"Probably a neighbor dropping off a casserole," Mark said.

"I hope she does take that trip. It will be a long summer if all she does is hang around the house."

We'd taken a couple of sips of our drinks when Susanna returned. To our surprise, she was accompanied by Barton's police chief. Bill Price was in uniform, a clear indication this was a business call. Mark and I set our glasses on the table, scrambled to our feet, and greeted him.

"Good morning, Ms. Walsh. Professor Burke." The chief gave us a gruff nod and a "get lost" look.

"Chief Price has a few more questions. I'm sorry—" Susanna gave a helpless shrug.

"No problem," Mark said. "We'll talk next week."

Susanna gave us each a hug and walked us to the sliding door. Mark and I went through the house in silence.

Police officers Tracey Brody and Ron Nicholstone stood beside one of the two police cruisers parked on the street.

"Hi, Tr...Office Brody."

The policewoman and I were well-acquainted thanks to my involvement in three murder cases. We had become friends and I called her Tracey, though not when she was on duty.

Tracey acknowledged us with a nod and brisk "Good morning."

The cruisers had drawn the attention of neighbor Vicki Shepard. She stood in her driveway with one of her daughters. "Is everything okay?" she asked before I could pose the question to Tracey.

"Everything's fine, ma'am," Officer Nicholstone said.

Vicki and the toddler walked across the grassy expanse between her driveway and Susanna's. "You were at the party last weekend. Gosh, it seems so long ago now. I'm still in shock about Derek."

The toddler pointed to Susanna's house. "No more come over."

"That's right, sweetie. Derek's in heaven now." Vicki stroked the girl's hair and gave us a helpless look. "I wish I could do something for Susanna. Something more than cook a few meals, bake cookies, and bring her garbage can up to the garage after the collectors have come by. My husband told her he'd be happy to help her with any big tasks she has around the house or yard."

"Those seem like small things, but they're very helpful," I said. I bent over and offered the girl a smile. "I'm Veronica and this is my friend Mark. Are you Josie or Eliza?"

"Josie!"

"The cracker snatcher." Vicki smiled. "Derek got a big kick out of her. That was the last time we saw him. I can't believe it." She shook her head and blinked a few times. "We were out here when he arrived home on Monday night. But he pulled right into the garage and went inside."

With a nod she indicated the wide curve in Susanna's driveway that led into the two-car garage under the house.

"I think Derek enjoyed our impromptu visits. We'll visit Susanna often and bring her some sunshine. Won't we, Josie?"

I kept my expression blank. From what Derek had said, he'd rather Vicki's kids had paid their *impromptu* visits on another neighbor.

"Yeah." Josie pointed at Susanna's front door. "P'lice."

"Brody. Nicholstone." Chief Price issued his brusque summons from Susanna's front stoop.

The officers snapped to attention and hurried up the driveway and into the house.

"Josie, hush!" Vicki grimaced. "I'm not getting a good feeling—"

"I'm sure everything is fine." Mark set his hand on my shoulder.

"Nice talking with you, Vicki. Bye, Josie." I wiggled my fingers at the tot.

"Go on swing!" The girl tugged on Vicki's arm.

Mark and I headed down the driveway. "Have fun!" I said over my shoulder.

I buckled my seatbelt and stole a final glance at Susanna's house. "Do you really think everything is fine?"

"I hope it is." Mark checked for oncoming cars and pulled into the street. "Maybe the chief has the autopsy results."

"But the medical examiner would give Susanna the results," I said. "And the chief wouldn't need two officers to come with him. Unless..."

"Don't even think it," Mark cautioned with a side-eye glance.

"Believe me, I don't want to."

Chapter Six

Mark and I didn't discuss Chief Price's visit for the rest of the afternoon, though it remained fixed in my thoughts, a worry in need of resolution. We stopped at the Food Mart on the way to my house and for the dinner we'd have with Carol and her husband, Patrick.

A few hours later, the four of us sat in my backyard, enjoying drinks and talk about summer plans while the grill warmed.

A tentative "hello" interrupted our conversation and made me turn in my seat—an Adirondack chair, of course. Tracey came toward us from the side yard. She was dressed in her "civvies:" jeans, a red T-shirt, and sneakers. Her brown hair hung loose to her shoulders.

"Sorry to intrude."

"Not at all. Please join us." I had several questions about her visit with Susanna lined up but kept quiet for the moment.

"May I talk with you and Mark?" Tracey's gaze shifted between Mark and me. "I won't take too much of your time, I promise."

Carol and Patrick hurried to their feet. Carol told Tracey not to rush. "We'll take a walk around the block to work up an appetite."

Tracey thanked them and took Carol's chair in our cozy seating cluster.

"Your visit to Susanna Rafferty's today wasn't a courtesy call, was it?" Mark sat forward, his posture straight and his attention fixed on Tracey.

"No." Tracey's tone turned grave. "Derek Morley didn't have a heart attack. We received the toxicology report this morning. It showed the professor had ethylene glycol in his system."

"Ethylene glycol?"

"It's in antifreeze and deicer fluid," Mark explained to me.

"And it's lethal. Even a small amount can cause seizures, coma, kidney failure. And death."

"Derek was poisoned?" I asked, incredulous.

Tracey nodded. "The ethylene glycol caused him to vomit. We think he got up to go into the bathroom—"

"Was dizzy and went in the direction of the stairs instead of the door," I finished. "Just what Susanna thought."

"Yes."

I asked, "You didn't arrest—"

"No. I collected the liquor bottles he used to make the Sidecar he was drinking when he fell ill."

The expensive cognac and liqueur Derek didn't share with his guests.

"We also collected other potential evidence," Tracey continued. "Professor Rafferty told me that you both attended a party at her home on Saturday."

I admired Tracey's quick redirect of the conversation. It was characteristic of the seasoned officer to offer a bit of information and then proffer more from us.

Mark responded. "We did. I'm sure Susanna told you she and Derek hosted our two departments' staffs and their spouses and partners."

"She did. How long have you and Susanna been colleagues?"

While Mark answered the several questions Tracey had about Susanna and his colleagues in the history department, my mind reeled over the news that Derek's death didn't have a natural cause. Someone with evil intent had prompted it and now the Barton police department had its fourth homicide case to investigate in less than a year.

And the fourth violent death that I've been connected to since my return to Barton. There's been more drama in my sleepy hometown than my fictional suburb on Days and Nights. *Truth is stranger ...*

Tracey drew me from my contemplation. "Veronica, you look deep in thought. Are you recalling something you observed at the party?"

"More like deep in shock. I was thinking about this being the fourth murder case in the village since I moved back." I paused. "I'm sorry, but I didn't see anything at the party that might connect to Derek's death. We had a great time. From my view, everyone got along within and between the two departments."

"It's possible no one from either department is the person who poisoned Derek." Mark looked from Tracey to me. "They use a housekeeping service. They have neighbors. There are any number of people who were in and out of the house who would have had the opportunity to poison the cognac or liqueur Derek mixed for a Sidecar."

Tracey's next question further struck a nerve and riled Mark. "What can you tell me about Derek's relationship with his wife?"

"Susanna? You can't suspect her!"

She had plenty of opportunities to slip poison into a beverage of her choice. Or Derek's cup of coffee or glass of water. I really don't want to believe that, though. Not Susanna!

"I have to ask the question." Tracey was calm and polite. "I always ask it."

"From all appearances, Susanna and Derek had a strong marriage."

"You've never heard rumors of an affair or—"

"Nothing." Mark's brusque tone underscored his reply. "Susanna has never indicated there was trouble between her and Derek."

Tracey's expression conveyed empathy. "I have to ask."

I had a question. "What about Susanna? She could've been the target. We're just assuming the poison was in Derek's liquor."

"Of course we're considering the possibility that the poison was intended for Professor Rafferty."

"Something did happen at the party." I shot Mark an uneasy look.

"I hate bringing it up, but…"

"But?" Tracey asked.

"The young children who live next door—the Shepard family—*crashed* the party. Just for a minute. They're very cute, but after they'd returned to their house, Derek said some not-so-nice things about their mother." I told Tracey what Derek had reported about Vicki's *research* on child behavior. "He had a lot of disdain for Vicki."

"All right," was Tracey's neutral response.

We talked for several more minutes, and she left.

"Was it horrible of me to *tattle* on Vicki? I can't imagine she would—"

"The police need to know everything." Mark patted my hand. "And you know by now that in a murder investigation, no one should be excluded from scrutiny unless they have an airtight alibi."

"Is everything okay?" Carol asked.

She and Patrick had come through the side yard and re-claimed their chairs. Mark and I traded glances. We could tell our friends the news before dinner or after dessert, or say nothing and let Carol and Patrick read all about it in the newspaper.

"Derek didn't have a heart attack. He was poisoned." Both Emersons gasped at my announcement. I told them about our visit with Susanna and Chief Price's surprise appearance. "The police think the poison may've been in the bottle of cognac or liqueur Derek used to make the Sidecar he was drinking when he died. She took those bottles and a few others to test."

"Ethylene glycol," Mark said.

"Antifreeze?" Patrick asked, stunned.

"You were at the house last weekend," Carol said. "Do the police think one of the guests is the poisoner?"

"It's a possibility." Mark addressed Patrick, a science teacher at Barton High. "How fast does ethylene glycol act once it's ingested?"

"Could be almost immediate. Within thirty minutes, or it could take a few hours for the body to react." Patrick shook his head. "If he had gotten help, he might have been saved."

"If the antifreeze was orange-colored, it would've blended in with the orange liqueur of the Sidecar."

Carol asked a follow-up question. "Wouldn't the drink taste funny? Wouldn't Derek have realized after one gulp?"

"Antifreeze has a sweet taste," Patrick said. "The taste would be masked by a sweet-tasting beverage, like soda or certain alcohols, like the ingredients of Derek's Sidecar. People need to be careful how they store it. Dogs and cats have died after drinking spilled antifreeze and kids, attracted by the color, have drunk it thinking it was soda."

Carol gave a shiver. "Horrifying."

Mark ended the discussion. "Why don't we get the burgers started before we lose our appetites?"

We agreed. The guys grilled the burgers and Carol and I went into the kitchen for the utensils, condiments, and salads I had bought at the grocery store.

"This must hit home for Mark. He had such a devastated look when you told us about the poison," Carol said.

I took the salads and condiments out of the refrigerator and set the bottles and bowls on a tray. "It's hard to fathom. Tracey asked us who was at the party. Half of the guests are Mark's colleagues. Now they're all suspects."

"I suppose Mark doesn't think any of them could be the killer?"

"Yeah. One big, happy family, though he didn't use those exact words."

"You've heard that before. And then the shock wears off." Carol pulled the tray of utensils and plates toward the edge of the counter. "The thought that someone Derek called a friend poisoned his beverage while enjoying Derek's hospitality."

"You know, it's possible the deed wasn't done during the barbecue. I don't know who else has spent time at the house over the last few days. Derek could've also had a tainted drink from another source. Maybe at Arden. Maybe a restaurant or quick-stop shop."

Carol nodded in agreement. "Could be." Her worried look deepened. "But what if a beverage in his home was poisoned. What if it was meant for Susanna?"

"I had the same question. Tracey said they're considering that Susanna was the target."

"Oh." Carol gave me a curious look. "Did Tracey ask for your help again?"

"Not yet. Maybe she won't."

My input into two murder cases the previous year had not been welcomed by the Barton police. There were moments when I thought I'd be arrested for interference. It was a surprise when Tracey, without the knowledge of the police chief, asked for my assistance at the start of the year when the director of the Barton Community Theater was shot dead. I had been in rehearsals for the theater's spring production of "Blithe Spirit" and, along with the show's stage manager, had found the director's body. Tracey took advantage of my proximity to the actors and crew—potential suspects—and requested my help. I solved the case, but Tracey made it clear I wouldn't be a regular crime-solving partner.

I picked up the tray with the salads and condiments and started for the door. Carol followed with the plates and utensils.

"But you're going to work on it anyway." Carol's plainspoken statement had an air of resignation.

"I don't think I can help myself."

Chapter Seven

Mark, Carol, Patrick, and I talked about more pleasant subjects for the remainder of the evening. After our friends had left, Mark and I stacked the dessert plates and coffee mugs in the dishwasher and returned to our Adirondack chairs. I brought along a pen and notepad. The flames in the fire pit on the edge of my patio were bright against the dark night and released into the air the delightful scent of burning maple wood.

"Let's make a list of everyone who was at Susanna and Derek's party." I took the cap off the pen and scribbled a few words at the top of the blank paper.

"Sidekicks once more." The warmth in Mark's voice and the sweet glance almost made me toss the pen and pad aside for a more pleasurable evening of holding hands by the fire.

We repeated the litany of names we had earlier recited for Tracey. After we finished, I asked if Mark remembered if Derek had had any issues with any of the guests.

"No, but that doesn't mean anything. There are always rivalries and resentments roiling under the surface. The academic world is a real-life soap opera sometimes."

"Does that mean professors sleeping with students isn't a stereotype?"

"It is a stereotype, but it does happen."

"Maybe Derek slept with one of his students and it didn't end well. Romantic revenge."

"Maybe."

"You know Tracey is going to go over their marriage with a fine-toothed comb. She probably already has a list of uncomfortable questions to ask." I veered the conversation onto a possible professional motive. "Was Derek challenged to be head of the department? Did someone else want the job and could still be bitter about not getting it?"

Mark rubbed his eyes and dragged his palm down his cheek. It had been a long, emotional day. "I don't know their department gossip. We're in a different building. If you want the dirt on the Sociology, English, or Economic folks—"

"You're the guy."

"Well, no." Mark chuckled. "No one would kill to be the head of the department. And it's a four-year term, so anyone who wanted the job would only have to wait another year or two for the position to become available."

"What if Derek wanted to continue?"

Mark gave his head an emphatic shake. "The chairperson is only allowed one term. There's not much prestige in it. More aggravation and headaches than glory."

"What would be typical headaches?"

"The chairperson mediates department disputes. The chair sets the department's class schedules, which means trying to accommodate everyone's preferences and knowing who's a *morning person* and who isn't. The chair has to enforce college and department policies." Mark's voice grew fatigued. "And does all this and more while also teaching classes and advising students."

"Have you ever been department chair?"

"Yeah. Susanna assumed the duties from me two years ago and has been excellent in the role. She's handled it with aplomb. The duties suit her and she seems to enjoy them. She has administrative skills I don't possess."

"Does she have aspirations for a higher position at Arden? Dean, maybe?"

"If she does, she's never voiced them. I wouldn't be surprised if she does get a plum position in the administration, but I'm not sure she'd want to stop teaching."

"What about Derek? I got the impression he'd relish a prominent position."

"He would." Mark was quiet for a few beats. "But the board of directors has been pushing for more diversity in faculty and administrative hires and promotions. More women and minorities. Hmm. That reminds me promotion and tenure announcements will come any day."

"Some good news for everyone at Arden to celebrate." I let a minute pass and then asked, "Does *anyone* on the list stand out?"

Mark sighed, leaned his head back, and studied the sky. To give him time, I counted a few of stars and watched the blinking lights of a passing plane.

"I can't pick anyone out of this lineup," Mark finally said. "I can't imagine anyone from History dumping antifreeze into anything in Susanna and Derek's refrigerator or liquor cabinet. I can't vouch for the folks in the psychology department, but I've always thought all of them decent people. I'm afraid one or both departments is about to be torn apart."

I clasped Mark's hand. "It will all be fine."

We intertwined our fingers and held each other's gaze.

"I hope so." Mark shifted his glance to the fire pit for a few seconds. When he brought it back to me, he had a grin on his lips. "You're having lunch with Miranda at an opportune time."

"Do believe I'll make the most of it. If I have to, I can re-direct the conversation to an entertaining antidote about a storyline from 1999 in which my rival was poisoned with arsenic. My character spent a month in prison before my lover forced a confession from the culprit."

"Who did it?"

"My rival's lover's stepbrother. It was a business decision."

Mark chuckled. "Makes sense to me."

Our conversation about poison and suspects ended. We sat outside for another hour, until the evening grew too chilly for the waning fire to keep us warm.

I later lay in bed, unable to sleep for all the thoughts swirling in my mind.

Was Derek's poisoning a business "decision" or was it related to his personal life?

With his professional and personal lives so connected, I had a hunch the answer to "Who poisoned Derek" would be a tangle too.

Chapter Eight

After we'd attended the ten-thirty Mass on Sunday, Mark had gone off with Patrick for a day of golf and an early dinner at a steak house near the golf course. I spent a couple of hours at All Things and then in the afternoon puttered around my yard doing a bit of spring cleanup. After tidying myself up, I went to my mother's house for dinner.

"Poisoning is so tidy." Mom set the bowl of mashed potatoes on the table and took a seat across from me. "Just pour it in a drink, inject it into chocolates, or stir it into a bowl of soup."

The mashed potatoes would be a good hiding place for poison. Cyanide. Arsenic. Perhaps hemlock or oleander? I shared my thought with my mother. "Or mix it into the mashed? If I didn't know you so well, those potatoes would've just lost their appeal."

Mom unfurled her white cloth napkin, spread it across her lap, and laughed. "The potatoes lost their peels forty minutes ago. And I'd never poison you. You're my only child and I'm counting on you to take care of me in my old age."

My mother, Nancy, was already in her "old age," according to the folks who administer Social Security, Medicare, and various senior citizen discount programs. She was closing in on eighty, though she looked, acted, and, according to her, felt, ten years younger than her actual age. She still went to work every day at Orchard Street Books, the shop she and my father opened in the 1950s.

"I don't think you'll ever reach old age. You're forever young at heart."

"It's because I haven't retired and never will. My work, my customers, all those books I read, they keep me young. Grace."

We said a blessing over our meal—roast chicken, mashed potatoes, and carrots—and filled our plates.

I speared a sliver of chicken and a slice off the end of a baby carrot and savored my first bite of Mom's comfort food. "Poisoning may be tidy, but it's also cold-blooded and premeditated. I can't imagine anyone from the psychology department *pouring* antifreeze into anything other than whatever container it goes into under the hood of a car. They're all so nice and kind. And the suggestion that Derek's wife did it. It's ludicrous."

"It is." Mom nodded. "But this isn't a case of a stranger breaking into their home to rob them and shooting Derek. Or a madman walking up to him on the street and stabbing him. This was personal. It was done by someone Derek knew." Mom paused over a forkful of mashed potatoes. "What does Mark say about the couple? Good marriage?"

"From all appearances. Mark doesn't have any gossip on them."

"Of course not. He's a gentleman. Talk to the women of the department. *Both* departments. Did Mark say anything interesting about Derek's professional behavior?"

"No. He blames it on distance. The history department is in a different building. If you want to know anything about the Sociology or English faculties..."

"Love those people."

I laughed, amused by Mom's droll remark. We enjoyed our meal for a couple of minutes.

"Innocence won't be proven with an alibi in this case." Mom cleansed her palate with a long drink of her ice water. "Susanna's an imbecile if she poisoned her husband and left the tainted bottle in her home."

Here was another opportunity to challenge one of Mom's assumptions. "Unless she thought it clever to leave the tainted bottle

43

because no one would believe she was stupid enough not to pour the beverage down the drain the minute the paramedics took away her husband's body. She could have even gotten rid of it before calling 911 and claimed Derek had finished the bottle."

"You've given this great thought. How was Susanna's mood at the memorial service?" Mom put a forkful of food in her mouth.

"Calm. No hysterical crying. Her voice didn't break once during her eulogy, but she was subdued and obviously exhausted. We can't take her composure at the service for an expression of guilt. A lot of people pull themselves together for the funeral and then collapse in private."

"True." Mom set her fork on her plate and took a sip of water. "I know you're going to get involved in this case and try to figure out who killed Professor Morley. Please keep this in mind, dear. Though the crime was committed in a non-confrontational manner, it doesn't mean the culprit is a non-violent person. Do be careful. Remember, you are my only child."

"I will, Mom, I promise."

Chapter Nine

A student in search of a small-town college with a picturesque campus need look no further than Arden College. Set on a thousand acres of well-maintained lawns, majestic trees of various species, and buildings designed in the Gothic style popular on many collegiate sprawls, Arden ticks the wish-list boxes of idyllic setting and excellent education.

I admired the scenery on the way to Hammes Hall, the classroom and office building where the psychology department was located. Two-stories tall and constructed of gray stone, Hammes anchored the campus's main quad on one end; gargoyles flanked its double-door entrance. I walked through a wide entry hall where several student paintings and sculptures were on display, took a left into another hallway where a dozen doors led into classrooms, and then another left into the stairwell.

I went along the second-floor corridor until I reached the open doorway to Miranda's office. She wasn't there. Derek's office was across from hers; his nameplate was still on the closed door.

Voices drew me a few doors past the office to the pantry and the gathering of Miranda, Bradley, Noelle, and two young women, one of them being the less-than-mournful gal who griped about having to hang around during the refreshment-portion of the memorial service.

Ashley, whose boyfriend had Susanna for an adviser.

Miranda greeted me with a wink and a teasing flash in her brown eyes. "Watch what you say, Detective Walsh has arrived."

Ashley's head jerked in surprise. "What?" Her pale cheeks took on a soft-pink hue.

"Veronica's here to have lunch with me," Miranda said, dismissing her wisecrack with a laugh. "We're going to talk about her stellar career."

"How interesting!" The second young woman thrust out her hand. "I'm Gretchen Smith. PhD candidate. Acting is such fascinating work. To spend hours every day portraying *another person* and doing it so well is remarkable. Were you a psychology major, by chance?"

"No, I studied Accounting as a second major in case I didn't succeed at acting."

"But you did succeed," Miranda said, "and now you're putting your degree to work at All Things."

Noelle regarded me with an astute look. Her silver-streaked black hair, which she'd worn loose at the barbecue, was gathered into a low bun. "You may not have come here on official clue-finding business, but I bet we're all under *your* observation."

"I wouldn't say you're under investigation, but now that you've raised the subject, I do have a few questions."

"I'll be the first to say I don't have any information to share," Bradley said. "Sorry. I can't see any of us wishing to harm Derek. He was my mentor and a good friend. And my steadfast supporter and guide through the tenure process."

Miranda and Noelle nodded in agreement of Bradley's declaration.

"Did the police interview all the faculty?"

"Yes. And a couple of deputies from the sheriff's department searched Derek's office here on Saturday. Noelle and I were present," Miranda said.

"What did they take?" I asked.

"Not much from his office. The most noteworthy item is the bottle of black cherry soda Derek kept in this refrigerator." Noelle gestured to the white refrigerator behind Bradley.

"Was Derek the only person who drank the soda?"

The five laughed. "Oh, yes," Bradley said. "He always had a Post-It on the bottle with his name written in all capital letters and a warning that no one was to help themselves to a drink."

"None of us wanted to help ourselves." Noelle made an exaggerated grimace. "Too sweet."

The soda's sweetness made it an excellent vehicle to mask the taste of the antifreeze and its dark color would conceal the neon shade of the poison.

"Do you share this pantry with other departments?"

"No," Noelle said.

"But anyone could've come in and tampered with the bottle," Ashley said. "Anthropology, Art History, and Political Science are in this building too."

"Yes," Bradley said, "but I don't think anyone from Anthro, Art, or Poly Sci had reason to poison Derek. I'm sure, though, that the police will consider the pantry's accessibility to everyone who works in the building and visitors. The doors are unlocked all day and there are no security guards at the entrances. Anyone can walk in."

Miranda agreed. "But someone outside the department would need to know Derek kept the soda in this refrigerator. It wasn't common knowledge."

But someone from outside the department who wished Derek harm could make an information-gathering visit to the pantry under the guise of getting coffee because their department's machine was broken or they were out of half-and-half and discover the bottle and Derek's note of ownership.

"Did any of you notice if someone from another floor or even a person who worked in another building came here last Monday? Someone who didn't have a reason to be on this floor?"

No one could think of an unusual visit to the department.

"Where did Derek eat lunch that day?"

"In his office," Gretchen said. "I stopped by for some advice on research I'm conducting. Derek was kind enough to discuss it with me over his chicken salad sandwich."

Noelle added, "He was here all day. No meetings."

"Did he complain of feeling ill? Stomach upset or a headache?" They all shook their heads.

"Sorry we're not helpful," Miranda said. "I can't imagine anyone in this department killing Derek. I have a feeling the only dangerous substance they'll find in his soda is sugar."

"Someone must have been in the house and had the opportunity to poison a beverage there. I don't mean anyone at the party..." Noelle paused. "Perhaps Derek had a visitor when Susanna wasn't home."

"The neighbor. The woman who kept pestering Derek about including her twins in a study. She's a possibility." Miranda took a step toward the door. "We should go, Veronica. I just need to grab my wallet."

We ladies followed her into the corridor while Bradley remained in the pantry to prepare a single-serve cup of coffee. Miranda ducked into her office, and Ashley and Gretchen headed for the staircase at the near end of the corridor.

I glanced at the stairwells at each end of the corridor. There was a fifty-fifty chance the poisoner—assuming Derek was poisoned on campus—didn't pass Miranda's office on their way to the pantry. I noted Bradley's office was on the same side of the pantry as Miranda's. He wouldn't have seen the approach of someone who used the stairs the two PhD candidates had used.

I made a final grasp for information, asking Noelle, "Was everything really hunky-dory among the staff?"

"We're like every other department on this campus. Really, like every other place of business on this planet. Including the world of soap operas. We have our own backstage intrigues and whispers. Of course there are rivalries and jealousies, but collegiality and a spirit of teamwork rule the day."

"We should trade stories some time."

"I'd love to." Noelle's quick smile faded. "What I'm saying is you'll find human drama everywhere you look. And just like everywhere else, you won't find a murderer. These professors may argue over theories and ideas and how to run the department, but they thrive on the discourse. No one would ever think to harm their debating partner."

Quite a diplomatic response. She can't exactly point an accusing finger right here in the hall. "What would Freud say about that?"

Miranda emerged from her office. "Freud would say that it's time for lunch. Ready, Veronica?"

Miranda talked about the horrors of poisoning on our way down the corridor and stairs. "I read stories about children and house pets drinking antifreeze and the fatal results. The kids think it's soda. The pets lap it up when it's been spilled on a garage floor. But what happens to the body after it's been ingested." Miranda gave an exaggerated grimace. "It's awful."

We crossed the front hall. Miranda pushed open one of the doors, and I followed her onto the sidewalk.

"You know ethylene glycol isn't only in antifreeze." Miranda established a brisk pace down the sidewalk. "It's contained in a number of household and automotive products. Adults need to be more careful of how they store this stuff to avoid these tragic accidents."

"I agree. But do you think Derek's consumption of the antifreeze was an accident?""

"No, I suppose not," Miranda conceded. "But I think it's jumping to a conclusion to assume it's murder. Someone may have only wanted to sicken Derek."

"Then why not put a substance in his drink that would make him sick but have no chance of killing him?"

"Like an overdose of a laxative?" Miranda asked. "Many

substances would alter the taste of the beverage so Derek wouldn't drink enough to get sick. I regret that I've learned more than I ever wanted to know about ethylene glycol in these last couple of days. Its sweet taste blends well with many beverages, like soda and the Sidecars Derek enjoyed. The whole thing is mystifying. Derek didn't have any enemies." Miranda clucked her tongue. "I make it sound as if Derek were a country and the poisoner an adversarial nation."

"People are rarely killed by an *enemy*. The killer is most often someone they know. A person they love and trust. In effect, the killer becomes an enemy in the last second, or hours or days, of the victim's life. You know that."

We walked in silence for a moment. I considered how Miranda had compared Derek and the person who had poisoned him to two combative nations.

"Perhaps Derek wasn't engaged in open hostilities with anyone," I said. "But was he involved in a cold war, so to speak, with a member of the department or someone at Arden?"

Miranda laughed. 'You mean a passive-aggressive relationship?' *Psychobabble.*

"If that's what you'd like to call it."

"Aren't we all involved in such relationships?"

"Well—"

"Here we are." Miranda stopped and gestured to a two-story brick building with two arched entryways and thick wooden doors that led into the student and public dining rooms.

Miranda held a door open for me. "No more talk about poor Derek. I want to talk about you and your glorious career!"

We went into the public dining room where food was served cafeteria-style and diners sat at wood tables in the center of the room. We selected our lunch—a turkey sandwich on a hard roll with lettuce and tomato for me, an egg salad sandwich for Miranda—and sat down at a table for two.

"Veronica, you're such a down-to-earth woman. How did you

not allow the awards, the spotlight, the fans' adulation to inflate your ego?"

"My mother would have burst my ego faster than you can say 'And the winner is.'"

Miranda tossed her head back and laughed. "In other words, you were raised well."

"Yes. My mother would agree."

"Did you plan on spending your entire career on the soap opera?"

I had taken a bite from my sandwich. I pondered the question while I chewed a mouthful of turkey and tomato. "No. I had dreams of stardom. Movies. Prime-time television shows. None of that materialized." I shrugged and dabbed my lips with a paper napkin. "I loved *Days and Nights*. It was a steady job, which made my parents happy. My character was an interesting woman I never tired of portraying. And the cast and crew were truly a family. That had great value to me since I'm an only child. I don't regret that I stayed there for thirty years."

"It was like a tenured academic position." Miranda gave a knowing nod. "Did you have a mentor when you started on the show? A veteran who showed you the ropes?"

"I did." I told Miranda about a co-star who was a founding cast member of *Days and Nights*. She was the matriarch of the show and an adviser and friend to me for twenty years until her death.

"Mentors are very important. Did you take any young actors under your wing and pass along your friend's wisdom? You must have. You're definitely the personality type who would."

I might be sitting in a public cafeteria eating a turkey sandwich, but I feel like I'm lying on a therapist's couch. I didn't know whether I wanted to laugh at Miranda's psychological profile of me or slap her across the face. I did take several actors under my wing over the years and told Miranda of how I had passed on my mentor's generosity and guidance.

51

"I'm interested in how fans become attached to the characters they see on television and think the actors are actually those fictional people. I know most viewers aren't delusional and that you, unlike your character, haven't been through multiple marriages—"

"My character, Rachel, was married *only* six times, three times to one particular man. I'm very sensitive about that statistic," I said with faux seriousness.

"Do forgive me. The vast majority of viewers know you are not the multi-wed Rachel. Did you ever, though, have to deal with a fan who didn't have a strong grip on reality?"

"You mean a stalker?"

Miranda nodded.

"I've never had a stalker. Thank goodness. A couple of my co-stars did and it was frightening. But they didn't believe the soap and its characters were real. They were just obsessed with the actors."

Miranda shivered. "That chills me."

She went on to ask more questions about my years on the soap opera, on the social significance of various storylines, and what impact Rachel's "life" had on my own. When Miranda finally paused for a few bites of her food and tipped her cup to her lips for a swig of her water, I turned the conversation back to Derek.

"You asked about my being mentored and guiding other actors. What about Derek? How many students did he advise this last year?"

"A few. I don't know the exact number." Miranda wiped her mouth with a napkin and busied herself with folding it and placing the neat square on her plate.

"Was Ashley one of his students? I saw her at the memorial service." *Unhappy to be there, I might add.*

"Yes, she was. I've agreed to be her adviser." Miranda shook her head in sympathy. "Ashley was a wreck over losing Derek."

"I'm glad everything's settled for her. Did Derek have a problem with any of his students? Anyone fail a thesis or dissertation or not graduate, for example?"

"Oh, no. Nothing so dramatic." Miranda laughed and wagged her finger at me.

"Anything less dramatic? Have any of his students complained about an unfair grade or tepid support?"

Miranda's mirth evaporated. "I'm not privy to Derek's relationship with his students. I have my own to manage. Are you ready? I should get back to Hammes. With Derek gone, I'm in charge of the department."

On the way out of the building, I asked, "Do you mean you're the department chair now?"

"Oh, no. I volunteered to step in and perform Derek's duties until a new chairperson is selected. Thank goodness we're between terms. The summer session is quieter and I'll be able to get my bearings." Miranda stopped outside the entrance and gave my elbow a light touch. "I enjoyed our lunch, Veronica. I hope I didn't talk both of your ears off."

"Not at all. I enjoyed it."

"I'm glad. I have so many more questions to ask. I'm curious about where Veronica ended and Rachel began. The process of creating and embodying a character fascinates me. How actors make their characters so real that viewers believe that you are that person."

"Me too," I said, laughing.

Miranda tilted her head and, with a coy smile, asked, "Can we meet again for another chat?"

"Sure." *On my turf.* "Why don't you come to my house this time?"

"Ooh!" She held her fist to her chest. "Will you let me hold your Emmy?"

"Of course."

Miranda twitched her shoulders. "I can't wait!" She turned on her heels and dashed down the sidewalk.

Chapter Ten

I longed to visit Mark in his office and share the details of the pantry chat and lunch conversation. We'd agreed, however, that I shouldn't drop by the history department while I was on campus. Mark didn't want his colleagues to think that I was there to dig for information or, worse, believe I considered them suspects.

I can call him and ask him to meet me here. We'll take a stroll around campus. I considered my suggestion for a few seconds. *I'll keep it for this evening.*

I pondered whether Miranda aimed to be the next head of the department on my walk to my car. *That's not a strong enough motive, though, for murder.* The position of department chair had a term limit; all Miranda had to do was wait for Derek's term to end and submit her name for consideration.

Gretchen sat on a bench outside the library, fingering the tip of the braid of her dark blonde hair. Flipping the long plait over her shoulder, she got up and walked toward me. "Did you enjoy your lunch with Miranda?"

"I did. We had a delightful conversation."

"Good. Miranda is *such* a brilliant woman." The widening of her green eyes punctuated Gretchen's admiration of the psychology professor.

Is Gretchen about to share a morsel of gossip on Miranda? Sing her praises and then smear her?

"Mind if I walk with you? You're going to the parking lot, I assume?"

"Yes. And no, I don't mind. Feel free to point out campus

landmarks and share tidbits of Arden history on the way."

We set off on a stroll's pace down the sidewalk.

"Professor Burke hasn't given you the full tour with insider information on Arden?"

What's she getting at with that cutesy tone? "Not yet. I've only been to campus a couple of times for events. A faculty reception and Derek's memorial service."

"It was lovely, wasn't it?"

"Yes. I didn't know Derek well. The eulogies gave me the sense that he was an admired colleague and teacher."

"He was." Gretchen's voice turned emphatic. "Derek was a terrific mentor to me. I'm heartbroken by his death and hope his killer is caught soon. I want that person brought to justice."

"I have confidence the Barton P.D. will soon solve the case." We walked a few yards in silence before I asked, "Do you want to tell me something you didn't want to mention in the pantry?"

"I'm sure it has nothing to do with Derek's death. But he and Ashley had a contentious relationship." Gretchen ended with an exaggerated sigh.

"Contentious? How? Was it over the direction of Ashley's thesis?"

"No." She hesitated. "Maybe I shouldn't say anything."

This one's a bad actress. Biting her lip and looking shy like I'm dragging the facts out of her and she's putting up a noble fight.

"Ashley's a great person. I've never had a problem with her."

"Sure." Worse than being a terrible actress, Gretchen was an inept practitioner of whatever psychological technique she was using to make me think she wasn't enthusiastically throwing Ashley under the bus.

"Ashley's focus is on the psychological development of girls and women—which is a terrific concentration—but Derek didn't think her scholarship met the department's high standard of intellectual excellence."

"Meaning he didn't support her doctorate thesis?"

"He did," Gretchen said in a half-hearted way. "Derek gave Ashley constructive suggestions to improve her research. Let's just say that Ashley didn't appreciate his efforts."

We turned onto the path that led to the parking lot. "So she didn't follow his advice?"

"No." Gretchen clicked her tongue. "A terrible mistake, in my opinion. Derek was a brilliant psychologist and an invaluable mentor. Ashley was lucky that he was her adviser and she should've taken advantage of the limited time she had with him to learn everything she could."

So defer to him? "That's a shame. But good mentoring includes giving the learner the space and encouragement to explore and test their ideas. If something doesn't work, it chalks up to a learning experience."

"I agree. But the purpose of an adviser is to guide the PhD candidate and share their wisdom. A balance can be struck between following the adviser's advice and experimenting with our own theories."

"That's true. So, did Ashley and Derek resolve their differences?" I asked, knowing the answer. Gretchen wouldn't have mentioned the troubled relationship if Ashley and Derek had made amends.

"No. They had a huge argument three weeks ago over a writing credit for a paper Ashley wrote and was going to submit to a journal. She refused to list Derek as a co-author."

"If Ashley wrote the paper, why would she—"

Gretchen shook her head and insisted, "Derek oversaw the project and consulted with her throughout the research. He deserved credit for his intellectual contribution."

"Was he given credit on all his students' articles?"

"Most of them. I *always* included him as a co-author. It was only right."

"Uh-huh." *Did students who gave Derek credit for their work get something in return? Glowing letters of recommendation? More money for their research?*

"Ashley threatened to file a complaint against Derek with the college."

"Did she?" I asked.

"No. Miranda convinced her it wouldn't be helpful. Miranda also volunteered to be Ashley's adviser, starting in July."

"So the conflict was resolved. Great."

We reached the entrance to the parking lot. Gretchen stopped and turned to face me.

"Yeah, but Ashley continued to sulk about it." The glance she offered me came loaded with meaning.

I didn't need a degree to understand her message. Ashley should be at the top of my suspect list.

Gretchen caught the corner of her lower lip between her teeth and her expression turned again into worried hesitation. "There's another thing."

"Oh?"

"Susanna and Derek had a party for their PhD candidates the Thursday before Derek died."

"That's nice."

"It was. But I overheard a conversation between Derek and Ashley's boyfriend when I went inside to use the bathroom. Kyle's in the history department. Susanna's his adviser."

"Uh-huh. What did you overhear?"

"Well, Kyle and Derek were in the dining room. I couldn't see them—"

And they couldn't see you, either, as you eavesdropped on their private talk.

"But I heard Kyle telling Derek,—'With all due respect,' he said—that he didn't like how Derek had treated Ashley and that he was glad Derek would no longer be her adviser."

"How did Derek respond?" I asked.

"He took no offense and said he was sorry if Ashley had misunderstood anything that he'd said and that his intention was always to help Ashley do her best work. He wished her well, both of them, he said."

"Sounds like it was all polite and the air was cleared."

"On Derek's part it was polite. He went back outside and Kyle walked through the living room and into the hall. He was heading to the bathroom and, quite loud, called Derek a vulgar name. If you know what I mean."

I said that I understood.

"And then, on Monday, Kyle came to Hammes at lunch time. I met him in the entrance hall. He said he came by to get Ashley. They were going to lunch in the cafeteria. I don't know why he had to come into the building and go up to the department. They could've met out front. Or at the cafeteria." Gretchen paused. "I thought you should know. Since you're very good at finding killers."

"Yes. Well... Thank you for telling me."

"Thanks for listening."

"Who's your adviser now?" I asked.

Gretchen's mood brightened. "Brad. He's terrific. He's been very helpful. I worried how Derek's death would impact my dissertation—I'm going into my defense year—but Brad has made the transition seamless and stress-free."

"Wonderful. What do you plan on doing with your PhD?"

"I'd love to stay here at Arden and join the faculty. This is home."

"Good luck. I hope you succeed."

I walked to my car with my head filled with more questions than when I'd arrived on campus.

Chapter Eleven

I wasn't done with Arden professors after I left the campus. In a case of perfect timing, one of the professors came to see me at All Things. I parked in the alley behind the shop and entered through the stockroom. Susanna stood by the checkout counter, talking with the boutique's manager, Claire Camden.

Claire noted my appearance. "Here she is!"

Susanna turned at Claire's gesture toward me. Her expression revealed relief. In a few long strides, she met me at my favorite spot in the shop: the candy counter at the rear of the sales floor. It was Claire's idea to sell sweets and she often rewarded herself for the brilliant suggestion by helping herself to one of the chocolates we kept in the display case.

I thought Susanna was going to throw her arms around me; her gladness at seeing me was palpable. Instead, she put a cool hand on my arm.

"I know you're a very busy lady, but can you spare a few minutes?"

"Of course." Shame on me for not adding that I wasn't a "busy lady" thanks to the hard work of Claire and my staff. If not for them, I wouldn't be able to take a long lunch break to discuss my former career. Nor would I have had the time to play sleuth in three past murder cases and now for the investigation of Derek's death.

Susanna seemed restless and I didn't think my tiny second-floor office would be a comforting venue for whatever she wanted to discuss. "Would you like to take a walk?"

"A walk would be good."

We walked to the front door in silence. I gave a quick greeting to a couple of our regular customers.

Susanna remarked on the encounter once we were outside. "Noelle was right about your effect on Barton's community of artists. Your support of them is invaluable. You should be proud of your accomplishment."

"I am. And you must experience fulfillment in your work when former students succeed in their careers."

"I do." Susanna offered me a smile. "It's particularly satisfying when a former student becomes a professor. It's always a thrill when I meet one at a conference and he or she is there to present a book they wrote or important piece of research they've done. It's the closest I'll get to being a proud parent. I'm an egomaniac, I know."

Our laughter relaxed Susanna. We continued down Orchard in the direction of the park. After a few seconds silence, I asked how she was "since Mark and I visited on Saturday."

"A visit interrupted by the police with news of the autopsy result. I can't reconcile it. The first jolt had sunk in and then bam! The news that his death was not by a natural cause was a gut punch."

We arrived at the park, and she gestured at a nearby bench.

"This is what I'd like to talk with you about, Veronica. You've proven yourself adept at identifying killers."

I've considered every person who was in our home over the last week of Derek's life and whether any were capable of killing him. I've racked my brain for a motive. I've drawn a blank." Susanna raised her hands in a display of despair.

"In my year of *identifying killers*, I've learned that everyone is capable of murder."

Susanna was quiet for a few moments. "I'm too close to this and can't see clearly. I've known these people for years. Our colleagues are like family to us. I can't be objective. You're new to the group. Except for Mark, you have no attachment or loyalty to any of us. You're clear-eyed. And observant. Will you be honest with me? Did anything happen at the party that seemed odd to you? Did anyone say or do anything that now makes you say 'aha'?"

"I've gone over your party in my mind, too, and nothing stands out. No red flags."

Susanna's frown indicated her disappointment. "I braced myself for that answer, but I hoped you might have noticed something."

"Sorry." I paused. "I had lunch with Miranda today. At the party she'd asked for an interview to talk about my career."

Susanna's mood lightened and a faint grin formed on her lips. "Miranda's a pip. She has an insatiable curiosity."

"I met her at the department's office and before we went to the cafeteria, we chatted for a few minutes in the pantry with Noelle, Bradley, Ashley, and Gretchen. Miranda mentioned that sheriff's deputies had searched Derek's campus office and had taken, among other things, the bottle of black cherry soda he kept in the pantry's refrigerator. She's confident no one in the department poisoned the soda. Did Derek ever confide in you any problems he was having with a faculty member or student?"

Susanna caught the corner of her lower lip between her teeth. After several seconds of thought, during which she watched a squirrel search the grass for its lunch, she looked up and met my gaze.

"You must understand there's always some tension between a professor and colleague or student. For a department chair, someone is always unhappy. Over the distribution of funds. How a policy is enforced or a dissertation or tenure review conducted. Students are under so much pressure to succeed. For graduate students, their whole future rides on their Master's or dissertation. It's a process fraught with emotion. Professors are very supportive and offer excellent guidance, but sometimes a hard truth must be told about the direction the student is taking with his or her research. Mark can tell you dozens of stories from his experiences."

I nodded in respect to Susanna's answer and then dug in for a more specific response.

"So there are people in the department with whom Derek had tension. Let's limit it to this past semester for now. Do you know whom Derek had disagreements with in the last month or two?"

"I can't name anyone specifically."

Really?

I concealed my frustration by keeping my expression neutral and suppressed a sigh. I didn't want pillow talk. I wanted the chat over dinner when news of the day was exchanged and work frustrations vented.

"Derek never voiced exasperation with a student who didn't take his advice? Or a colleague with whom he butted heads?"

Susanna, visibly uncomfortable, shifted on the bench. "I can't think of anyone who would be so angry with Derek that they'd want to kill him!"

I sympathized with the roiling mix of emotions Susanna was experiencing and her reluctance to accuse the people who were offering her comfort, but I needed her to whittle down the large cast of suspects to a few persons of interest. "Susanna, you said you can't be objective, but you need to be. If you want the person who poisoned your husband punished, if you want justice for Derek, you need to be frank with me."

Susanna sighed. "The truth is...at the party you saw how Derek could be. What he said about our neighbor. He didn't suffer fools. Not that Vicki is a fool. But Derek thought..."

"He must have resented Vicki's intrusion into his personal time. People were probably always suggesting psychological studies that he should conduct."

Susanna offered me a thankful look. "I can't give you a short list of names who might have poisoned Derek. He could have angered any number of people merely by focusing his critical eye on their work or behavior. Derek was a psychologist. He was always evaluating others' behavior. Even mine! He couldn't help himself."

Fantastic. A large cast of suspects it will be.

Glad I had kept my purse and not stashed it under the counter at All Things, I pulled out a pen and pocket-size notepad and flipped through a few pages in the pad to find a blank sheet.

"You said you've made a mental list of every visitor to your home in the week before Derek died. Who are they? You don't need to name the people who attended Saturday's party."

Because Mark and I have already assembled and discussed at length that guest list.

"All right."

Susanna exhaled a breath that implied a heavy burden had been lifted from her shoulders. "On the Thursday evening before the barbecue, Derek and I hosted a dinner for our graduate students. It's a tradition we started years ago. We enjoyed mingling the two departments. More than one romance has started at those gatherings."

The barbecue that Gretchen mentioned. I nodded and jotted down the names, including Ashley's and Gretchen's, Susanna recited without indicating I'd been told about the gathering less than an hour earlier.

"Did you sit inside or out on the deck?"

"The deck. It was a crisp evening, but Derek lit the fire pit so we were all comfortable. You're not going to ask me who went in the house during the party, are you? I can't possibly remember!"

"I wasn't going to ask. I suppose nothing happened that sticks out in your mind?"

Did Derek tear apart one of the attendees' thesis or dissertation in front of the group? Do a verbal takedown of someone's research project?

"Nothing. We had a terrific time."

"Did Derek have a difficult relationship with any of his students?" I didn't I wouldn't mention Ashley's accusation, unsure whether Gretchen had exaggerated the matter. If Susanna didn't mention it, maybe it wasn't a big deal. Or maybe she didn't know.

"Anyone unhappy with the guidance he gave on their research?"

"No. Derek had strong relationships with his students. There was much mutual respect among the group."

I recalled that at the barbecue, Derek hadn't put the bottles of cognac and liqueur on the beverage table for his guests to enjoy. *He probably didn't share with his students, either.* But I asked, "Did you have a beverage table for everyone to help themselves? Could the cognac—?"

"No. We only served soft drinks. Even though all the students are over twenty-one, Derek and I chose not to offer alcohol."

"Good decision. Who else visited your home?"

"We use a cleaning service. Two women come on Wednesday mornings."

"Were either you or Derek home when they came that week?"

"No. We were both on campus. Derek never even met the women, but the police have interviewed them."

"Okay. Any other visitors?"

"No."

"No one visited Derek when you were out?"

"Not that he mentioned," Susanna said.

"I assume you gave these names to the police."

"I did."

"The cognac and liqueur Derek drank. Do you know when the bottles were opened?"

"I don't. But they were both at half-full when I gave them to the police. I can't believe we're having this conversation. It's surreal." Susanna took a tissue from the pocket of her jeans and dabbed her eyes with it. "Do you have any more questions?"

"Not right now."

"Thank you, Veronica. I trust the police, but I'm thankful for your help. I think you may be able to uncover helpful information the police can't. People seem to be very open to you."

"I'll do my best."

We left the park and strolled back to All Things.

"You mentioned on Saturday some of your plans for the summer. Do you have anything else lined up for the next three months?" I asked.

"I have plenty of work to do on a writing project, if I can pull myself together to focus on it. I also want to pack up the books in Derek's home office. Friends have told me not to make any big decisions for at least a year, but I have no need for Derek's psychology books—though I'll keep one or two for sentimental reasons—so I'm going to give them to the department. It will be a good start to letting go."

We stopped in front of All Things. "Maybe you'll find a book or two on his shelves that deal with grieving and loss." I placed my hand on Susanna's shoulder in a gesture of comfort. "Help from Derek, in a way."

Susanna's eyes grew moist and she pressed her hand against mine. "I'm sure I will. Thank you, Veronica. I feel better for talking with you." She hurried to the next corner, crossed Orchard Street, and went into the deli.

I imagined a secret compartment in one of Derek's books—a text on criminal psychology or psychopathy, perhaps. A chunk of paper cut from dozens of pages to create a hiding place for...what? A love letter from a mistress? A blackmail note? An empty vial containing a thin film of antifreeze?

Clever way to get rid of evidence. The police probably won't flip through Derek's books for clues.

I snickered. "I should have offered to help pack the books."

I went into All Things, where Claire stood near the front of the shop. With a light touch she used a feather duster to clean the table display of carved wooden figures of black bears, foxes, moose, and other Adirondack wildlife.

"How was lunch? She whisked the duster over the ears an adorable bear cub.

"Delicious." I headed for the stairs to the shop's second floor sales area and my office.

Claire fell in step beside me. "You had a serious look on your face out there on the sidewalk. Penny for your thoughts? I'll need a second to get one out of the cash drawer."

"I was trying to figure out how I can ransack Derek's home office for clues while his wife is standing right there."

"Maybe she'll help you."

I unlocked my office door and went in; Claire closed the door behind her and dropped into the visitor's chair in front of my desk. She wasn't being forward or nosy. Claire had been my confidant, even a sidekick, on two of the murder cases I'd solved. She was one of my suspects—we joke about it now—on the first murder case I was involved in—the death of my next-door neighbor, who had at the time was the owner of All Things and therefore Claire's boss.

"I assume Susanna just asked you to find her husband's killer."

"Yes. She asked if I'd noticed any suspicious activity at her party last weekend." I dropped my purse in the file cabinet behind my desk and sat. "Which I didn't."

"Does she have any ideas about who may've poisoned her husband?"

"No one and everyone." I related my conversation with Susanna.

"Maybe she's hesitant to accuse anyone because she has a guilty conscience." Claire's eyebrow, the same shade of copper as her hair, arched. "Susanna is on your suspect list, right?"

I nodded. "I like her, but I can't assume she's innocent."

"Don't be fooled by a possible grieving widow act. Did you learn anything at Arden?"

"Two sheriff's deputies searched Derek's office on Saturday and took away the bottle of black cherry soda he kept in the department pantry's refrigerator."

Claire sat up straighter in her chair. "It would be easy for someone to go into the pantry and pour the antifreeze into the bottle. Just to the office early and be the last to leave."

"Or switch out the bottle Derek put in the fridge with a bottle with the poison in it," I said. "The person had plenty of time to replace the poisoned soda with the original bottle Derek had put in the fridge. He died Monday evening and the toxicology report didn't come back until Saturday."

"Susanna had plenty of time, too, to replace a poisoned bottle in her home."

"This is true." Our observations made me feel dejected. "I bet the results on all the bottles tested will be clean. No poison."

"You'll still figure it out. You always do."

"Three times. That's all."

"That's a streak." Claire grinned and her dark-brown eyes conveyed pride in my "achievement."

I appreciated the regard Claire had for my sleuthing skill. I paid her to manage All Things, not play detective with me and boost my ego. I wouldn't admit that to her, however. She'd ask me for a raise.

"What about the professor who invited you to lunch?"

"Miranda Liu. She was more interested in my career than in talking about Derek's. She's taken charge of the department. Makes me wonder—"

"If she was Derek's rival?" Claire asked.

"Yes."

"Hmmm. You said Susanna had gone to a meeting and found Derek dead when she came home?"

"Yes."

"What if Derek had a visitor while she was out? He was on the deck when the visitor came. Derek went inside to get them a drink and the killer poured the poison in Derek's glass."

"It's a possibility. Though it may have been too much of a risk. Derek could have caught them putting the poison in his glass."

Claire got up and put her hand on the doorknob. "Be careful, Veronica. You now have a reputation for solving murders and everyone knows you'll be investigating this case. Keep an eye on your beverages." She opened the door and disappeared into the hall. Her warning, an echo of my mother's, hung in the room and chilled me to my core.

Self-served water might be my beverage of choice until the case was closed.

Chapter Twelve

After closing All Things, I went across Orchard Street for dinner with Mark at the Hearth. We sat at a table near the cold fireplace and swapped accounts of the day's events.

Mark had heard about the search of Derek's campus office and the black cherry soda bottle taken for testing. "It goes without saying it was the talk around campus. Did Miranda have anything to add?"

"No. She was more interested in my years on the soap. When I got a question in, Miranda just glossed over it with babble."

Mark chuckled. "Psychologists want to talk about everyone but themselves."

We paused when our server brought my ginger ale and Mark's beer. We did our routine clink of our glasses and sampled our drinks.

"I met two of Derek's PhD students. I'd seen one of them—Ashley— at the reception after the memorial service." I described the sulky behavior I'd observed. "And I learned from the second student—Gretchen—why Ashley wasn't fond of Derek. Derek didn't approve of Ashley's academic focus on women's psychological development, yet when Ashley wrote an article she was going to submit to a journal, Derek demanded she list him as a co-author." I filled Mark in on my walk-and-talk with Gretchen.

"Intellectual contribution?" Mark gave a mirthless laugh. "Shame on Derek for pulling that nonsense."

"Yeah. I didn't dare mention it to Susanna."

"Susanna?"

"Yeah. Maybe I should've started with her visit. She was at the shop when I got back from lunch. She wanted to talk."

Mark registered surprise. "About what?"

"She asked if I'd noticed anything unusual at the party. Susanna thought some kind of odd behavior would've stood out to me because I'm new to the group. She said she can't be clear-eyed about who may have poisoned Derek."

"Of course she can't."

"And Susanna can't think of anyone who would want to harm him. But when I pressed, she admitted he could be a pill—my word—and everyone he worked with could've had an issue with him. She asked me to help find out who poisoned Derek."

"Did you tell her you've already started work on it?" Mark, amused, asked.

"No." I sipped my ginger ale. "What if Derek made things difficult for Ashley after she complained? Sabotaged her work or threatened her future in the world of psychology." My theory gained form with my assumptions and embellishments. "And Miranda, regretful that she talked Ashley out of filing a complaint, is protecting her! Miranda might even believe that Derek had it coming to him."

"That's farfetched."

Our server approached, set our salads on the table, asked if we wanted anything more, and left with the assurance we had all we needed.

"You're suggesting Miranda is covering up a crime." Mark spoke in a low tone, his focus on spreading ranch dressing over his salad.

"Ashley may have only intended to make Derek ill. Payback for being so difficult."

"You're spinning big assumptions." Mark, his expression skeptical, took a bite of a ranch-drenched lettuce wedge.

We put the conversation on hold for a few minutes and enjoyed our food.

I then continued to make my case. "Miranda's worked with Derek for several years. If Derek had a problem with Ashley, he might have had a problem with other female students. Miranda could have a lot of evidence against him. Derek might've even harassed her." I had a moment of clarity. Or perhaps absurdity. "This might mean Miranda has a motive too. She's in charge of the department now. She seems more pleased than distraught, under the circumstances."

Another dubious look from Mark. "You're weaving quite a story. Your time in the soap world still has a strong hold on you." He finished with a grin and chomped on a cherry tomato.

I returned volley with a smile and a quip. "Perhaps the killer will make a Freudian slip and out themself." I waited a beat. "And then there's Ashley's boyfriend, Kyle–"

"Kyle Wettig?"

"I guess. Is there more than one PhD Kyle? Susanna's his adviser."

"Yeah. That's him."

I related the snippet of Ashley and Kyle's conversation I'd overheard at the memorial service.

"Ashley's mood is understandable. If she and Derek had a difficult relationship, the last thing she'd want to do is give up a Friday night to attend his memorial service. And it's typical of Kyle to make the best of things. He's a bright-side kind of guy. Earnest. Decent."

"Except there's an instance when he wasn't." I told Mark about the party Derek and Susanna had hosted for their students and related the conversation between Derek and Kyle, as recounted by Gretchen. "Kyle could have poisoned Derek to exact revenge on behalf of his girlfriend."

"You can't be serious."

"If Ashley poisoned Derek, I'd expect her to conceal her dislike for him at his memorial service. Put on a sad face and don't pout by the coffee urn. Act like Kyle."

"Who behaved as he always does."

"Maybe they're playing mind games!" I seized the idea and ran with it. "Ashley acted like a sourpuss to make people think she didn't poison Derek, because the killer wouldn't be so obvious. And Kyle was all conciliatory because who would suspect the nice guy."

"And they saw you at the service, know your reputation for solving crimes, and staged their conversation to make you jump to that conclusion."

"That's a great point!" *Did the couple play a mind game on me? Did I fall victim to the maneuverings of a pair of conspirators?*

Mark's smirk indicated his *great point* was said in jest.

"Am I psyching myself out?" I asked, chagrined.

"No." Mark set his fork on his plate and reached across the table. He placed his hand over mine. "It's wise to put all the theories on the table. Separate the chaff from the wheat."

"You're a generous man. You know, Kyle could've poisoned Derek's liquor at the student party. After he talked with Derek."

"But Derek mixed several drinks since Thursday," Mark said. "He would've gotten sick before Monday."

"True. I saw him mix a drink on Saturday. Unless there was a second bottle of liqueur that he didn't use until Monday. Or something..."

"Yeah. Or something."

"You mentioned your colleagues knew about the police search of Derek's office. Did anyone share a theory on who poisoned him?"

"No. Everyone's been circumspect and keeping their opinions to themselves. Maybe they've discussed them in private, but no one mentioned their suspicions to me. It could be because I'm with you and your crime-solving reputation precedes you."

"Faculty lounge talk not meant for the outsider's ear. How clubby."

"Noelle put up a defense for them all and said the department has the typical drama every workplace has. The professors thrive on debate—"

"As we do in History. Intellectual stimulation and all that."

"I get it. Noelle also told me that, just like everywhere else, I wouldn't find a murderer in Hammes Hall. But *someone* killed Derek. There is a murderer roaming around."

"Of course Noelle will defend her staff. They're her friends."

"Still, I'm disappointed that she didn't have anything to share. The administrative assistant always has all the gossip."

"You're typecasting," Mark said.

"How does a cliché become a cliché," I countered. "Look, we're debating!"

Our server arrived with our entrees. By unspoken agreement, Mark and I ended all talk about Derek, suspects, and drama in the halls of academia.

Chapter Thirteen

"Telephone call, Veronica."

"Thanks. I'll take it in a moment."

Claire conveyed the message to my caller and set the shop's cordless phone on the candy counter. I finished packing a pound of chocolates, secured the box with string, and handed the box across the counter to my customer, with warm thanks. I waited until the woman walked away to take the call.

"Good morning, Ms. Walsh. This is Ashley Monico. We met yesterday."

"Hi, Ashley. And please, call me Veronica. How may I help you?"

"I'm working toward my PhD in Developmental Psychology and am writing an article on women's psychological development and well-being."

"Sounds interesting."

"Thank you. You've had a unique career. If you're willing and have the time, I'd love to talk with you about your experiences in daytime television and the impact playing a fictional woman had on you. Do you have time to sit for an interview? It will only take an hour or so."

An opportunity for me to ask Ashley my own set of questions! "I'd be glad to be a part of your research, Ashley. Your questions should be better than any soap magazine ever asked."

Ashley laughed. "I can come to Barton for the interview."

She makes that sound as if Barton is five hours from Arden and she's making a huge sacrifice. "Terrific." I gave her my home address, we set a meeting time for the next day, and ended the call. Lowering the phone to my side, I gazed into the shop and pondered the debut of my latest role: Research Subject.

From soap magazine interviews to a psychology research project. I'm glad people still want to talk with me, but do I want to be analyzed by a psychologist-in-training who's anxious to make her mark in the field? What if she concludes I'm full of neuroses and delusions and details every single one in her paper? Will she think I'm vain and insecure because I need help being a natural brunette? Or will she decide I'm uninteresting and leave me out of the article? Embarrassing!

"What was that about?" Claire wandered over from a display of blown-glass crafted by a local artisan.

"A grad student from the psychology department wants to interview me for a research project."

"What's her topic?"

"Women's careers and their psychological development."

"Neat. I wonder if she'll use your name or refer to you as Subject A or a phony name like Penelope."

I shrugged. "I don't know."

"If you sense she's going to write that you had debilitating depression when your soap was canceled and you lost your will to live—"

"I didn't."

"She might exaggerate to support whatever point she wants to prove."

"She doesn't have a point to prove. That's the purpose of her research. To find out. But I'll tell her to call me Claire C."

"You're so funny." Claire looked heavenward in a show of faux exasperation. "I assume you're going to *interview* her about Derek while she interviews you."

"Of course I am. What do I look like, an amateur?"

"Well, you are. Or has Barton P.D. put you on their payroll?"

75

"Not yet. And I won't hold my breath that they will. But back to Ashley. A fellow PhD candidate shared interesting information with me yesterday." I told Claire what Gretchen had said about Ashley as we crossed the sales floor.

"Ooh, possible motive!"

"Yeah. I can't wait to talk with Ashley one-on-one. And I'm going to pay a visit today to Derek and Susanna's neighbor. If she took Derek's rejection of *studying* her twins hard—"

"Then it was bye-bye, Professor."

"I'm counting on her having good information she's willing to share."

We parted at the front of the store. Claire headed to the register and I went upstairs to my office.

I was glad to be a part of Ashley's research and to help the young woman earn her degree. Our interview would also assist my research project, for I had my own degree to earn: a PhD in Sleuthing.

Chapter Fourteen

"Do you have a few minutes to chat?"

"About Derek's death, I suppose? Sure." Vicki opened wide her front door and invited me inside.

Like Susanna's home, Vicki's was a center-hall Colonial but very different in decoration. A small collection of toys was piled next to the front door. From my vantage point at the front door, I spotted a dollhouse, play kitchen, and three toy trucks in the room where, in Susanna's house, hung the curious framed print. The living room had a sectional couch, two chairs, and no breakable objects, busts of presidents or psychiatrists, or artwork that would teach the home's young residents a bit of American history. On the other hand, no artwork meant none of the youngsters could "restore" the paintings with crayons or grape juice stains.

"I'm not interrupting lunch, story hour, or nap time, am I?"

"No. The boys are at school and the girls at daycare." Before I could string together a non-offensive way of asking if she had a job, Vicki offered the answer. "I work part-time in the town clerk's office. I got home from my half-day a little while ago."

"I'm sorry. I'm sure you want to relax, not answer questions from nosy me."

Vicki started down the hall. "No problem. I have time before I have to pick up the kids. But I don't think I'll be much help. I didn't have a lot to say to the police."

I glanced at the photos on the walls in the passage to the kitchen. A portrait of each of her children when they were newborns surrounded a large photo of the family standing in a pile of leaves.

"Would you like a drink? I have diet soda, apple juice, milk, water. I can make coffee, if you'd like."

"Water is fine."

Vicki indicated for me to take a seat at the island. Spread across the black marble were coloring books, loose crayons, several sippy cups, four cereal bowls—a few milk-soaked Cheerios were in one bowl—a couple of chunky board books, and a plastic cup half-filled with orange juice.

"I'm sorry about the mess. Mornings are a frenzy around here." Vicki set a bottle of water and a glass at my place.

"Thanks. You have a beautiful family. Well worth the frenzy."

She came around the island and sat on the stool two over from mine. "I'll miss the chaos when the kids are old enough to do things for themselves." She flipped open a can of diet Coke and took a deep sip from it. "Josie and Eliza picked a few flowers from our garden yesterday and brought them over to Susanna."

"Sweet. Were you home last Monday when Derek fell ill?"

Vicki nodded and swallowed a mouthful of soda. "I was reading the girls a story when the ambulance came. My husband went over to see if he could help. We're horrified that we didn't hear Derek fall down the stairs or yell for help."

"Did you see Derek when he arrived home?"

"Yeah. The girls and I were out front, watering the flowers. The boys were running around out back. Derek waved as he pulled up the driveway. He didn't stop to talk, so I can't comment on what condition he was in."

"What about when Susanna got home?"

"I didn't see her. We went inside soon after Derek came and we were in for the rest of the night." Vicki gathered the loose crayons and dropped them into a plastic container on the counter.

"So you didn't notice if someone came to visit Derek before Susanna arrived home? You didn't hear him talking with anyone out on the deck?"

78

"No." Vicki stacked the board books and coloring books and turned to me. "It's so noisy around here, a bomb could go off in the backyard and we wouldn't hear it."

I offered a half-smile at the hyperbole. "Have you recently overheard Susanna and Derek arguing or having sharp words with each other?"

Vicki took a sip of her soda. "No. Never."

"Have you noticed either Derek or Susanna coming home, recently, during the day for, say, an hour or two?"

"You mean for lunch?"

"Yeah. Or—"

"A quickie?" Vicki grinned.

I, who participated in dozens of love scenes in my three decades on *Days and Nights*, was embarrassed. "Well—"

"I never saw them come home for lunch and a bit of romance."

"What about just one of them coming home in the middle of the day? With, umm, a companion?"

"Oh. No! I never saw that. Susanna and Derek were a solid couple. They'd never cheat on each other. I hope Susanna isn't a suspect, because she was so devoted to Derek."

I agreed. "Did anyone in the neighborhood have a disagreement or dispute with Derek? Neighbors can argue over many things. A fence. A tree that sheds leaves on another's property. Loud teenagers—"

Vicki snorted. "That may have been our problem ten years from now. But no, we're a quiet neighborhood and we all get along. My kids don't respect property boundaries yet, you've noticed. They're always running into Susanna and Derek's yard and the yard on the other side of our house. Never a complaint from anyone. The neighbors look out for each other's kids. Derek and Susanna did too."

I drank some water. "Derek mentioned research—"

Vicki's eyes flashed. "Yes. I had proposed a research project that my kids would participate in. Two projects. One on the girls. The title should be something like *Twin Life in the Twenty-first Century*. And another on the siblings of twins. What's it like to have siblings with such a strong, almost supernatural bond. I think those would be important studies. Did Derek tell you about my videos?" Vicki shifted on her stool to face me. "There are these challenges parents do with their kids."

Vicki described the video. "Eliza has better impulse control and patience than Josie." She giggled. "You can watch all my videos online." She blurted the name of the social media site where she posted the videos.

"I'll check it out. It sounds like you did all of Derek's work for him."

Vicki laughed. "Almost. He just had to write the paper."

I finished the water and slid off the stool. "Thanks for your time. You don't have much of it for yourself, so I appreciate it."

"That's okay. I really wish I could be of more help." Vicki followed me to the front door. "I wonder if someone who worked with Derek poisoned him. A professor or maybe a student ticked about a bad grade."

"Yeah. Maybe."

I walked to Susanna's at a slow pace to have time to consider what Vicki had said. In her view, she and Derek were partners in a sure-to-be groundbreaking research project. In Derek's opinion, Vicki should be the subject, not observer, of a study.

"And he told her to put her phone down and parent her children and not indulge her insecure ego," I murmured.

So someone lied. Or were Derek's words a tease, a show for whatever reason?

"Was he afraid one of his colleagues would steal his idea?" I doubted it.

Or was Derek testing for their reaction? Seeking approval for the project before he agreed to work with Vicki? Nope. Derek was too experienced to require his fellow professors' approval. And his ego was too healthy to need their endorsement.

Susanna met me on the front stoop. "I saw you go next door. Standard procedure in detective work or do you suspect Vicki of poisoning Derek? Because I can't imagine."

Susanna closed the front door and we went into the living room.

"Both." I sat on the opposite end of the couch from Susanna. "Vicki said that Derek didn't have a problem with any of the neighbors. No ongoing disputes. True?"

"Yes." Susanna gave her head an emphatic bob. "Derek got along with everyone."

"Even Vicki and her husband?"

"Of course!"

"What Derek said at the party, about Vicki's videos of the kids and how she should stop putting them to the ridiculous *challenges.* He said that a paper on Vicki and her parenting skills would be more interesting than one on her children. Vicki told me that Derek was very interested in writing two papers on her family." I repeated Vicki's proposed research studies. "And you said he was joking about his scorn for Vicki and her pop psychology. I'm confused."

Susanna slouched, leaned her elbow on the arm of the couch, and massaged her forehead with her palm. "I don't know if Derek really said all that to Vicki. He'd sometimes claim that he'd done something outrageous but he hadn't. Maybe he did say it but didn't mean it or maybe he was making a joke at the party for laughs."

"Did he say anything to you about writing the papers?"

"No. He wouldn't have written them. He would've thought writing a paper on the Shepard children presented a conflict of interest."

"Why wouldn't he have said that to Vicki instead of insulting her or leading her on? If he said what he said or she said he said."

We laughed over my tongue twister. Susanna said, "Derek was too honest for his own good sometimes."

"How long before you got home on Monday did Derek arrive?"

"I guess forty-five minutes to an hour."

Enough time for Vicki to invite Derek over for a drink with a splash of antifreeze and conversation about their joint research project. Or to invite herself over to his deck sanctuary.

Perhaps she called the drink a peace offering.

I didn't like where my suspicions led me. Vicki was a mother of four young children. She worked her butt off both in her home and for the village. To think she might have poisoned Derek because of some insult he might not have even said was disgraceful.

This was the part of amateur detective work that I detested. It made me suspicious of everyone. We all have disputes with others, we've all muttered "I could kill" in a moment of anger, and many who would never take action have entertained in their minds how they would take someone's life.

I studied Susanna—another nice person I suspected—and reminded myself that of the more than one dozen people I'd suspected in my short "career" in sleuthing, they were all innocent except for three. The fact made me feel worse.

Why couldn't you limit your work to finding lost pets? Or better, focus all your attention on All Things? Go for Barton Businesswoman of the Year!

I pressed. "What is Vicki's husband's work?"

"Jordan's an engineer and devoted to his family. I don't know where he gets the energy to work all day and come home and race around the yard with the kids."

Could Jordan have poisoned Derek in a chivalrous act of revenge on behalf of his wife? I considered the possibility in the silence that fell between Susanna and me.

I doubted Jordan had poisoned Derek all because of an insult.

A punch in the jaw would have been more satisfying. Thought what if something else was going on between Derek and Vicki?

"That's a serious look." Susanna straightened in her seat.

"Have you thought of something important?"

"No, just thinking. Have you watched Vicki's videos of the kids?"

Susanna clicked her tongue and made a dismissive gesture. "They've never been on my to-do list."

Chapter Fifteen

Business at All Things was in a lull when I returned from Susanna's, so I went up to my office and did a bit of research in preparation for my interview with Ashley.

I went to Arden's website and read the press release on Derek's death—no mention of it being of unnatural causes. I selected *Academics* and then *Departments* to land on the psychology department's page and a link to the roster of faculty members. Derek was still in the lineup; I clicked on his name and was directed to his page and a short professional biography and a list of his recent publications.

I scrolled through the bibliography, noting the article titles and journal names. Derek had co-authored many of the articles. Of these articles, women were the first author of ten and men four.

"Hmmm...Did Derek demand writing credit more often from women—his female students—than from men?" I wondered aloud.

I returned to the faculty list and clicked on Miranda's name. Her list of publications numbered more than two dozen. She was the first writer on fifteen of the publications. First authorship on other articles was evenly split between men and women. More impressive was her position as president on the board of the Association of Asian American Psychologists and research on the mental development of Asian American children.

Bradley's biography listed several appearances on cable news and public television programs and a few video links to lectures he'd given around the country, including a talk for a popular nonprofit organization that hosted presentations by leaders from every field and industry.

I took a cursory glance over the biographies of the other psychology faculty and then navigated to the history department's page.

After reading Susanna's credentials and impressive bibliography, which include a Pulitzer Prize and National Book Award for her biography of Eleanor Roosevelt, I went to Mark's biography and lingered over his faculty photo. He was a handsome fella, with his still-plentiful sandy hair, green eyes, and warm smile. What really made Mark a hottie, though, were his kind heart and generous spirit.

"I'll see *you* later."

"Talking to yourself again?" Claire stood in the doorway. A teabag dangled from the mug she held.

"Research." I closed Arden's website and felt the heat of a blossoming blush fill my cheeks. *For crying out loud, you're a fifty-plus woman admiring the age-appropriate man you love, not a co-ed called out for a crush on a professor.*

"So, what did the neighbor have to say?" Claire sat in the visitor's chair and set the mug on the desk. She swirled the teabag around the steaming water for a few seconds.

"The standard line. Everyone in the neighborhood loved Derek. No one had a problem, blah blah. Susanna said the same. I wonder if he'd visited with Vicki when he got home Monday evening. There's a discrepancy between what Vicki told me today, what Susanna's said, and Derek's sarcastic remarks about Vicki at his party." I told Claire about the two research papers Vicki thought Derek would write about her family. "Did Derek lead Vicki to believe he'd write those articles? Did he not commit to a study, but she jumped to the conclusion he would? Did they never discuss the papers and Vicki is lying? Or deluded?"

"Delusions of grandeur." Claire took a sip of tea. "She envisions herself a brilliant, self-taught psychologist."

"She saved a lot on student loans."

Claire fingered the teabag's label. "Maybe there was *something* going on between Derek and Vicki and this research talk was cover."

"An affair between the two has crossed my mind. But it seems ridiculous."

"Why?"

"There's at least a twenty-year age difference—"

"That's never stopped anyone."

"Derek's attitude toward Vicki was dismissive."

"More cover. Act like there's no attraction."

"Vicki has four kids under the age of seven. She's too tired to have an affair."

Claire arched her brow. "Maybe an affair energized her. Derek made her feel attractive. Like a woman."

"I'm sure her husband does. They do have four kids."

Claire raised her mug to her lips. "Do any of the kids look like Vicki's husband?"

"Claire!"

"Why not?"

For a minute she occupied herself with drinking the tea, and I gave more consideration to the possibility of Derek and Vicki conducting an affair under their spouses' noses.

It would be a very bold move. Very soap opera. And if Derek had fathered the twins, it would definitely be a conflict of interest to conduct research on the pair. Stop! But could he and Vicki have? Vicki works part-time. Maybe Derek did come home at lunch hour and they...

In the same way I had to suspect innocent people of murder, I also had to consider all motives and scenarios, no matter how farfetched they seemed. I left my mind open to the possibility of a Derek—Vicki illicit union.

I typed Vicki's name in the browser's search box and opened the link to her video page. "Want to watch videos of Vicki's kids?"

Claire pulled her chair to the side of the desk, and I positioned the laptop so we could both see the screen. I opened the video titled *Candy Challenge.*

"This is the *experiment* Derek told us about at the party."

Vicki shot the video at her kitchen island. Josie and Eliza sat side-by-side, their hair again in pigtails and each clutching a sippy cup. This was my first up-close view of both girls; I at once noticed the subtle differences in their facial features that helped distinguish one from the other. I knew Josie from her slightly pointed nose. Eliza's eyes were a bit rounder than her twin's and there was a timidity in her blue eyes compared to Josie's paler, and sharper, blue eyes.

"They're cuties," Claire said.

Five M&M candies were placed in front of each girl and Vicki, from off-camera, said, "Mommy's going to the laundry room for a minute. Don't touch the candy until Mommy comes back."

Josie set her cup on the table and, with one hand still wrapped around it, slowly moved her other hand toward her short line of candy.

"Josie, wait until Mommy comes back. Don't eat the candy." Vicki's voice was a bit farther from the camera than when she first spoke.

"Mine!" Josie rested her hand a centimeter from her candy.

"Don't eat the candy until Mommy comes back!" I guessed Vicki was by the door that opened to the basement stairs.

Josie shifted so that her legs were under her and she leaned over her candy. Her glance moved several times between the camera and the M&Ms. Eliza observed her sister's movements. Josie put her finger on the center candy, a green M&M.

"What's her name?" Claire asked.

"Josie. She's the one who crashed the party and tried to eat a whole plate of crackers and cheese in two stealth moves. The other is Eliza."

Eliza gave Josie a side-eye. "Mommy say wait!"

"We'll call her the Enforcer." Claire giggled. "Or maybe Family Snitch."

Josie popped the green candy in her mouth. She chomped on it for a second and did the same with a red M&M.

Eliza sat on her knees. "Mommy say wait!" Her tone was urgent.

"Here comes Mommy!" Had Vicki observed the pair from the top of the basement stairs or had she really gone down to the laundry room?

Josie grabbed two of Eliza's candies and placed them with her diminished portion. Eliza screamed and tears sprang from her eyes. She reached for her stolen candy and earned a slap from Josie.

The scene drew an acerbic remark from Claire. "Did Josie forget about the camera or does she think her mother will forget how many M&Ms she gave each of them? Or maybe she just doesn't care."

Vicki's voice drew closer. "Eliza, did you eat two M&Ms? Mommy told you to wait."

"Josie ate! Josie ate!" Eliza's red-cheeked agony and tear-choked exclamation broke my heart.

"Josie, did you eat Eliza's M&Ms?" Vicki's authoritarian tone, I believed, was for her audience.

I returned to Vicki's main page at the same moment Claire said, "Turn it off. That's not cute."

"No. Poor Eliza. I understand the shots Derek took at Vicki."

"Eliza needs to learn how to throw an elbow or her sister is going to dominate her their whole lives. Josie will copy Eliza's homework, steal her boyfriends, and grab the spotlight whenever it shines on sweet Eliza." Claire returned the chair to its place, picked up her mug of tea, and moved to the doorway. "It's been fun slacking off from work."

"I'll be down in a minute," I said to Claire's back as she stepped into the hall and out of my sight.

I looked over the titles Vicki had given her other videos and clicked one labeled *Halloween Tricks.* I watched a few seconds of her and her husband telling their two boys that they'd accidentally thrown out all their Halloween candy. The boys, like their sister Eliza had done in the candy challenge, dissolved into tears. I closed the browser and my laptop.

Like Claire, I understood Derek's criticism of Vicki. I bet if a professional psychologist treated her children the way she did in her videos, Vicki would demand the person's license be revoked and sue for millions.

Rather than thinking Derek was too harsh in his assessment of Vicki, I wondered if he'd been too mild. Had he understated what he'd said to her and been more critical to Vicki than he admitted? Or did he embellish his account to entertain his guests? Did Claire hit the mark and Derek and Vicki were having an affair and his disdain for Vicki was an act to hide his adultery?

Tracey stopped by my house after her shift ended and we didn't compare notes. I told her what I'd learned, but she didn't share the information/evidence the police had gathered in the case. Typical good cop behavior, though it drove me mad.

"Gretchen put a mark on both Ashley and her boyfriend's backs," I said, shifting my Adirondack chair to face Tracey's. "I assume she told you, too, about Ashley and Derek's not-wonderful relationship."

"Yes, she and others from the department mentioned that they didn't have the easiest professor-student relationship."

"Do you think it gives Ashley or Kyle a strong motive for poisoning Derek? Kyle did confront Derek at the student party."

"I'm not going to put a mark on their backs," Tracey said with care.

"I bet they're suspects," I retorted. "Along with the entire psychology department and every department in Hammes Hall."

"I wouldn't say everyone."

"I assume the Anthropology faculty are safe."

"Fascinating people, those anthropologists."

I snickered. "I wonder if Vicki Shepard ever asked any of them to *study* her children. What it's like to be a human twin. I paid her a visit today. Didn't learn much, except she thinks Derek was fascinated by her children. Have you watched her videos of the kids?"

"Oh, yes."

"Claire and I watched them this afternoon. Amazing. And not in a good way."

"I agree." Tracey gave me a serious look. "Some parents are diligent about keeping their children off social media. No photographs, no videos. And then other parents put their kids on display. Why do you think that is?"

"The parents think their kids are super-special. The most remarkable children in the history of children. Or, more likely, the parent needs attention and validation."

"Bullseye," Tracey said. "I can't imagine your mother was like that when you were a kid. No demand that you be the star of every school play."

"Absolutely not! She and Dad made me double major in Business and Theater in case the acting thing didn't pan out. They always supported me, but were forever practical. What about your parents? What did they think about you becoming a police officer?"

Tracey's expression lit up. "Supportive, just like yours."

"So no mommy or daddy issues between us. Our friends in Hammes Hall would say we're boring."

Tracey laughed. "I'm fine with that assessment."

Two squirrels chasing each other around the back of my yard distracted me for a few seconds. "If Derek told Vicki her daughters would have mommy issues..."

"I'd imagine she wouldn't like that," Tracey said.

"Of if he'd concluded that Ashley must have a daddy issue

because she didn't follow Derek's guidance..."

"She'd be understandably angry."

"Angry enough to punish the rejected *father figure*?" I asked.

Tracey laughed. "You've become quite the student of psychology, Veronica."

"But how am I doing in my Introduction to Criminology class?"

"Very well." Tracey rose from her Adirondack chair in a graceful move I envied. "Keep up the good work."

"See you around campus, Officer," I said to my departing friend.

Chapter Sixteen

"What a cute house," Ashley said of my folk-Victorian when I welcomed her the next day. "Beautiful curb appeal."

I kept a snappy "Is real estate your back-up plan if the psychology thing doesn't work out?" from slipping from my lips and instead asked, "Have studies been done on the psychological impact a well-kept house and lawn have on potential buyers or is it simple common sense?"

'I think it's a no-brainer." Ashley laughed. "A study would be a waste of grant money."

"If only our government had the same attitude about spending our tax money." I held the screen door open. "Is how to secure grant money and manage it a required class for graduate students?"

Ashley stepped into the hall. "No, but it should be. I'll toss it in the suggestion box."

With the humorous icebreaker dispensed, we moved into the living room. I had one final quip. "I feel like this is a test I haven't studied for."

"No pressure." Ashley made herself comfortable on the couch and her glance took in the room. "I'm the one who has to prove my thesis." The red hue of her hair was more pronounced with it now hanging loose to her shoulders.

"I'll do my best to help you succeed at that."

She offered me a grateful smile and began the interview. She had composed a list of thoughtful questions I'd never been asked in the dozens of interviews I'd done over my career.

"Did you study psychology to shape your character and

understand her behavior?"

"You were fresh out of college when you landed the role. Did your character's development influence your own development through adulthood?"

"How did the treatment of female soap characters change over the course of your career? Did you have to fight for your character to be more confident and independent? Did you have conversations with writers and producers about your character's psychological development?"

"The lines between the fictional character and the actor are often blurred for viewers. Was the line ever blurred in your mind between your real self and the woman you portrayed?"

Thirty minutes into the interview, she hesitated after I'd talked about jealousy among the *Days and Nights* cast. "It sounds like you handled it well when someone envied your success. Were you ever..." She hesitated.

"Do you want to know if my hazel eyes ever turned green with envy? Let's just say I have typical human reactions to life events."

Ashley giggled. "And we'll leave it at that. How much time fell between the network's announcement and the last day of filming?"

"A few weeks."

"What was your reaction? You must've had a range of emotions. The classic five stages of grief?"

I glided my fingers over the sudden outbreak of goose bumps on my arm. "Oh, yeah. For a long while I was sure I'd land another role. Reality slowly sank in that I wouldn't."

"Because of your age? And because you're a woman?"

"Well, yeah. A bigger part was that there are fewer soaps on television now and that means fewer parts for all actors."

Ashley scribbled several sentences on a legal pad. "How did you feel about not being able to get a job because of age and gender discrimination and the dearth of roles?"

"I wouldn't call it discrimination. That's just the way the

business works. From soaps to prime time to feature films."

"A man in his sixties with a love interest twenty-five years younger. But you'd been nominated several times for a Daytime Emmy award and won one. You should've been valued for your achievements and outstanding work, not devalued because you're a woman over the age of fifty. Your co-star Alex Shelby didn't have a problem finding a new role."

Ashley had done her research. Alex, my leading man on *Days and Nights*, was also a fifty-something but had no problem securing a role on a soap filmed in California after our show's cancellation.

"True." I made a helpless gesture. "What can I say."

Ashley nodded, serious, and dropped the line of inquiry. She went on to ask more probing questions about my state of mind and actions in the weeks before and after the final taping of *Days and Nights*. "How lucky that an opportunity for something completely different came so soon after you returned home," she said after I related the story of my neighbor's death and my subsequent purchase of All Things.

"My temporary homecoming became a permanent one and I couldn't be happier." I emphasized the last word so it would be clear to Ashley that the sudden end of my acting career hadn't done irreparable damage to my self-esteem or altered my identity.

She flipped through the few pages of notes she had written. "Thank you very much for this interview, Veronica. You've made a valuable contribution to my research."

"Good. Your questions were excellent. I think I'll reflect on them for a long time."

"If you think of anything you'd like to add to my notes, give me a call."

"I will. So, what do you plan to do after you've earned your PhD? Do you want to teach at the college level, go into the corporate world, or maybe a private practice?"

"Well, I planned on becoming a professor." Ashley sighed. "But now I don't know if the academic life is for me."

I steered the conversation with care. "Higher Ed isn't what you thought it would be?"

Ashley shrugged. "I thought it would be more collegial. For lack of a better word."

"I suppose there's a lot of competition for grant money and to publish research before someone else does."

"Yeah. There's that. Everyone's out for himself. Publish or perish."

"It was the same on *Days*. Some of us were content to spend our entire careers in the soap world. Look at me, I was on *Days and Nights* for three decades. But there were actors who had their eye on a prime-time show or film career. Usually a young actor who had limited acting experience who'd chew the scenery and campaign for more airtime and beefier storylines. They competed with everyone. One even dared be disrespectful to Melanie Hughes."

"Wow!" Ashley said, her eyes growing wide at the notion of someone dissing multi-Emmy winner Melanie, whose success and popularity on *Days and Nights* had gained her fame beyond the boundaries of the land of soap operas.

"The young actress was a huge diva."

"Care to name names?" Ashley winked. "Just between us."

"Sorry. I'm not a gossip, though you probably wouldn't recognize the actress. She thought she'd be a big star. She spent two years on the soap and was on a cable show for four years, but she hasn't landed a notable role since that show ended." I paused. "Divas aren't unique to show business or the college theater department. Does the psychology department boast one or two superstars in their own mind?"

Ashley drew a tight spiral in the wide margin at the top of the legal pad. "Yeah." She raised her glance and met my steady gaze. "Another person Derek advised thinks she's already a full professor the way she critiques everyone else's work, from their research idea to the final paper. She would've used a different research method or she would've included another group in the survey or she wouldn't have pursued the topic at all. And gets a thrill from pointing out typos and grammatical errors."

"Annoying." *Gretchen?*

"She wants a position in the department after she gets her PhD. She'll probably get it. She's one of those people who're only out for themselves."

"I've known a few of those types."

Ashley continued. "She won't speak up unless she's the main beneficiary. I had an issue…"

I waited for Ashley finish the sentence.

Ashley sighed and named names. "Derek and I didn't have the best adviser-student relationship. He didn't agree on how I want to focus my research and thesis on female psychological development. And then, when I wrote a terrific paper and was preparing to submit it to journals, he demanded I give him a writing credit! All because he was my adviser!" Ashley paused, a look of disgust clouding her expression. "There are more women than men in psychology graduate programs—"

"I didn't know that. Interesting."

"We're equal in number at Arden. I didn't expect the other women in the PhD program to stage a protest for me—a sit-in in Derek's office or anything like that—but I thought there'd be more of a public unity behind me. You know what I mean?"

"I do."

"Some encouraged me in private and told me that they'd discussed the situation with their adviser. They thought the adviser—Derek's colleague—had more leverage to get Derek to be a better mentor. I don't know whether those professors talked with Derek before we had the blowup over the writing credit. One PhD candidate didn't back me—" Ashley hesitated.

I offered help. "Gretchen?"

Ashley nodded. "Yeah. She talks a good game about women succeeding and helping each other thrive, but when it came to solidarity for me, she kept her mouth shut. She didn't want Derek to start treating her the way he treated me."

I clicked my tongue in sympathy. "I'm sorry. There will always be someone who puts their own interests first. I hate to say it, but a lot of women are only out for themselves. They work their way to the top and then don't give a hand to help other women."

"They feel threatened," Ashley said. "They don't want other women to rise to the top faster than they did."

"Yes. It's all jealousy. So don't let Gretchen's lack of support discourage you."

Ashley, her expression solemn, nodded.

"I'm glad everything has worked out for you. Miranda is your adviser now."

"Yeah. Thank goodness for Miranda."

Do you have any more questions for me?"

Ashley gave a shy smile. "May I see your Emmy award?"

On my walk to All Things, I pondered Ashley's experiences with Derek, his claim to her hard work—her intellectual property—left me steaming mad and Ashley with plenty of motive to kill him.

But Miranda had agreed to be Ashley's adviser starting with the upcoming semester. Ashley would no longer have to contend with Derek.

I returned to my theory that Ashley may have only wanted to sicken Derek. She had her freedom from him, there was no reason to kill him in order to switch advisers. Did an unintentional heavy-hand in pouring the antifreeze into Derek's drink turn Ashley into a killer?

Gretchen's lack of support for Ashley also angered me. *When she's a professor, will she be an adviser in Derek's mold? Use others' work to elevate herself and diminish the work that she doesn't agree with?* What did Gretchen gain by siding with Derek? Was she someone who didn't want to jeopardize her own degree and career by speaking truth to power, or did she and Derek have more than a professor-student relationship?

I reached the corner of Orchard Street and Sycamore. "I'm confused!"

I wanted to talk with Susanna and Miranda about the relationships between Derek, Gretchen, and Ashley, but I didn't have time that day for the conversations. I had to get back to work at the shop and my canasta club was to gather that night for our weekly game.

"I have enough to hold up my end of the conversation, for sure."

Chapter Seventeen

"What a difference a week makes!" Sandy Jenkins uttered the exclamation in place of a welcome when she met me at the door of Ella and Madeline Griffin's Victorian home on the north end of Orchard Street. "Thank goodness an autopsy was done on the professor or someone would've gotten away with murder."

Sandy led me into the parlor—the octogenarian Griffin sisters preferred the old-fashioned term for "living room"—where Ella, Madeline, Myrtle Evans, and Dotsie Beattie were already enjoying a pre-dinner cocktail. When Sandy offered to pour me a drink, I requested a ginger ale.

The five ladies and I formed a group that met each week to play canasta. I was the newest member of the club and its youngest participant; I'd been invited to join a year earlier after Dotsie's partner had passed away. I was paired with Sandy because Dotsie doubted my canasta-playing skill. Each week we gathered in a different member's home and shared a meal before the cards were shuffled and dealt.

"Spill what you know." Dotsie slid to the center of the couch and patted the cushion she had vacated.

I sat, took a sip from the glass of ginger ale Sandy handed me and related most of what I'd so far learned.

Of course, sex was the first thing the widowed, seventy-something Dotsie mentioned. "I think the probability is high that either Derek or his wife was stepping outside the marital boundary line. One lover or another could have spilled the poison. His. Hers. Or Susanna. Is she a merry widow?"

Dotsie's blue eyes blazed with interest. The spunky woman enlivened our card games and often took conversations in odd directions.

"Not at all!" I thought of my mother's query on Susanna's demeanor at the memorial service. "There were plenty of tears in her eyes when she asked me for help."

"Tears can be easily manufactured," Sandy said. "You know that better than anyone."

"But you're not the only actress in town." Dotsie turned sideways to face me. "Maybe she's trying to act rings around you. See if she can do it."

"But Veronica is the best actress." Sweet, soft-spoken Madeline punctuated her review of my talent with a firm nod.

Ella voiced the week's common refrain. "Susanna had the best opportunity to poison her husband."

Myrtle corrected the eldest member of our group. "*Multiple* opportunities. If I were Susanna, I'd have killed him with small doses of arsenic over the course of several weeks. Months, even."

We were so accustomed to Dotsie's off-the-wall declarations that none of us was shocked by Myrtle's matter-of-fact delivery.

"You've spent a lot of time thinking about this, Myrtle," Sandy said, her tone wry. "Or did you at some time or another plot to kill someone?"

"The former, I pray." Madeline pressed her hand to her bosom.

"Let's all admit we have at some time or another," Dotsie paused and gave Sandy a look, "fantasized about killing someone."

"Not I!" Madeline protested.

"I *killed*," I made air quotes, "a couple of people on the soap. That was enough to stop me from considering it in real life."

"I've wanted to kill slobs who throw their garbage in the street, don't clean up the mess their dogs leave on other people's lawns, and the people who are paid to keep public restrooms clean but don't do the job properly!" Sandy, a professional housekeeper who held the world title of Most Immaculate Cleaner of Everything in perpetuity, gave an emphatic nod. "But not literally."

"I wanted to throttle a woman who stayed here in 1985," Ella said. The Griffin home had been, for decades, the Barton Inn, a family business established in the colonial days, later re-opened by the Griffins' parents, and then managed by the never-married sisters. "What a fussy, spoiled, arrogant person she was."

"I remember her." Madeline's pucker indicated she perhaps didn't think the best of everyone.

"What about you, Myrtle?" Dotsie glanced at her canasta partner.

"There's been a client or two."

Here was an opportunity to gather potential evidence. Myrtle, a well-connected insurance agent, had provided me helpful information in the past.

"Is Susanna your client? Do you manage her and Derek's insurance needs?" At the previous week's card game, Myrtle hadn't said that the couple was a client, but Derek's passing wasn't a topic of conversation because his unnatural cause of death wasn't yet known.

"No. They're not clients. And I don't know who handles their insurance."

"That makes it harder to find out if the professor had a huge life insurance policy or if Susanna recently took out a policy on him." Dotsie rattled the ice cubes in her glass and took a generous swig of her drink.

"The flip side is Susanna was the target and Derek the wrong victim. The poisoner could have gotten their preferred beverages mixed up." Sandy set her glass on the table beside the chair.

"Or," Ella said with emphasis, "someone poisoned Derek to exact revenge on Susanna."

"You took my husband so I'll kill yours!" Dotsie chortled.

"The great tragedy is it might all have been a juvenile act."

Myrtle got up to freshen her drink. "If his grad student poisoned him for revenge, she's an idiot. Her whole career would be over before it's begun."

"She could have given him a nasty review at the end of the semester," Sandy said.

"She should have filed a complaint with the college. Professors will continue their shenanigans and abuse their authority until they're held accountable." Dotsie spoke with rare seriousness.

Sandy offered another dose of reality. "Then Ashley would be labeled difficult. A complainer."

"So Miranda Liu saved Ashley's academic career. Perhaps *she* exacted the appropriate revenge."

I responded to Myrtle's remark with a reference to Dotsie's earlier crack. "Miranda seemed rather sanguine on Monday. Rather merry."

"A work wife!" Dotsie revved up again.

Myrtle added a touch of scandal. "And maybe more."

"And now a merry work widow." Dotsie poked my shoulder blade. "Maybe they liked to *psychoanalyze* each other."

Myrtle snorted. "Or perhaps this other student, Gretchen, enjoyed some *extracurricular* activity with the professor."

"My goodness!" Madeline pressed her hand against her pink cheek.

Dotsie made another point. "Maybe Ashley and Derek had something going on and he threw her aside for tattle-tale Gretchen. And that's why Ashley is suddenly upset about having to slap Derek's name on her articles."

"I give Ashley a lot of credit," Sandy said. "Even if she didn't file a formal complaint, she was brave to speak up for herself and her work. It's disgraceful she was alone in the fight. The other women in the PhD program should've stood up with her."

Dotsie said, "Maybe Gretchen realized her failure to support Ashley. In an acute case of the conscience, she put a dose of girl power in Derek's soda!"

"That would be quite a *punch*," Myrtle quipped.

Dotsie added, "Her support of Derek may've all been an act to benefit herself. But when the semester was over, she pounced."

"Or punched," Sandy said, giggling.

I sipped my drink and wondered what Arden's psychologists would make of my joining this wacky band of canasta players in the wake of my *traumatic* life event? Would they say I'd needed a group to replace the "family" I'd lost with the soap's cancellation? Had I accepted the invitation to join the club because I needed social contact? Or was I a glutton for punishment?

Psychoanalysis, indeed.

Chapter Eighteen

I received a text from Tracey the next morning.

T: Coffee break? I'm in the alley.

It wasn't time for a break. All Things had been open for twenty minutes. I was the shop's owner, however, and could take a break whenever I wanted. I headed for the alley behind All Things.

"There wasn't a trace of ethylene glycol in any of the bottles we took from the home and the department refrigerator." Tracey told me a minute later. She leaned against the driver's door of her police cruiser and took a generous drink of coffee.

I cradled the cup of coffee she had bought for me at the bakery. "Did you take the fingerprints on the bottles?"

"Yes, we pulled the prints, for the record. What do you have for me?" Tracey gave me an expectant look.

I suppressed both a look of surprise and a triumphant grin. Tracey, unlike in previous murder cases, had neither ordered me to stay clear of the investigation nor asked in explicit terms for my assistance. She knew, without a word exchanged, that I was "on the case."

"I had my interview with Ashley yesterday."

"How'd it go?"

"She plumbed the depths of my psyche. I understand myself so much better."

Tracey laughed.

I told her how I'd worked in a few questions and elicited a few answers about her relationship with Derek. "But you already know the full details."

"Yes. You know we conducted our own interview with Ashley."

"And you know she was at the dinner for Derek's and Susanna's students the Thursday before—"

"Yes."

"And..."

"And it's one of many facts we've collected in the case." Tracey sipped her coffee.

I sighed as if every burden of the world lay on my shoulders, folded my arms on the table, and rested my head on them.

"And the Emmy goes to..."

"It better be me," I said.

"Of course."

"So you won't tell me anything about your interview with Ashley. Is there any evidence that the poison was intended for Susanna?"

Tracey shook her head. "Nothing. It's one theory. Susanna said that no beverages were finished between the day of Derek's death and Saturday. According to her, everything in the refrigerator that was there on Monday was still there on Saturday. Milk, orange juice, coffee creamer. If Susanna was the target, the beverage would've still been in the house when we collected the containers on Saturday."

"Unless the poisoner visited between Tuesday and Saturday morning and removed the poisoned bottle."

"What a tangled web."

"No literary references," I said. We don't need another Arden department involved in this case."

We laughed and lapsed into a short silence, during which we sipped our coffee.

"Any hints of an extramarital affair by Derek or Susanna?" I asked.

"None so far. Yet another avenue to pursue."

I hope that avenue leads nowhere. "What about the next-door neighbor, Vicki?" I related my visit with her. "Am I a terrible person for suspecting a mother of four little kids?"

"No. I was trained to suspect *everyone.*"

"So you don't declare someone innocent simply because they're clean cut, or a doting mother, or even a devout person?"

"Exactly. Or by their position in the community, high or low, or the amount of money in their wallet. The sweet old lady can be guilty and the smart-mouthed teenager can be innocent."

"Have you ever had a case where a sweet old lady and a smart-mouthed teen were both suspects?" I enjoyed the sudden levity in our conversation. "Maybe even accomplices?"

"No."

"Will you call me when you do?"

"With your involvement in cases this last year," Tracey said, "they're likely to be *your* suspects. Will you call me?"

"Haven't I always?"

"Hmmph."

"So Vicki is a legitimate suspect. But *is* she a suspect?"

Tracey gave me a side-eye and tossed her empty coffee cup in the dumpster. "Keep in touch." She got into her cruiser and pulled out of the alley.

I remained for a couple of minutes after Tracey left and contemplated what she had told me.

What had been the poisoner's reaction when Derek's death was announced? Was it a "Holy bleep, I didn't mean to kill the man," or "Holy bleep, it worked!" It was no surprise that none of the bottles the police tested contained ethylene glycol. The ease with which Derek's mystery beverage was poisoned and the tainted bottle "disappeared" frightened me.

In the three previous Barton murders, the killer had confronted the victim and committed a terrible act of violence. A blow to the head, a stabbing, a shooting. This fourth killer moved with stealth, never giving Derek an opportunity to fight for his life.

Chapter Nineteen

"I'm so glad you called!" Susanna threw her arms around me and gave me a breath-taking squeeze. "I've been wandering around here, talking to myself. I'm starting to get answers. Forgive my appearance." She gestured to her gray T-shirt with Arden's insignia printed across the chest, jeans, and tennis sneakers. "I'm packing Derek's books." She waved at the open door to Derek's office.

"Need some help? We can talk and pack."

"Your assistance would be much appreciated, along with your company."

After she topped off her glass of water and poured a glass for me, we went to Derek's office, where the print of the man standing before a mirror still hung in its frame beside the mahogany desk that was positioned in front of the windows facing the side yard. The wall opposite the front window was concealed by a built-in, floor-to-ceiling bookcase. Two of the case's shelves had already been packed, the books stacked in three cardboard boxes on the floor under the front window.

I took a closer look at the print and read the attribution below the image. Belgian artist René Magritte had painted *Not to Be Reproduced* in 1937. I squinted to make out the title of the book lying on the mantel under the mirror.

"*The Narrative of Arthur Gordon Pym of Nantucket*," Susanna said. "By Edgar Allan Poe."

"That's a mouthful. Fascinating painting. It reminds me of the image of Narcissus gazing on his own reflection in the water. So, what's with this guy?" I jutted my chin at the painting's dark-haired man. "Is he a modest fellow? Not in love with himself? Did he not shave that morning? Does he have a big nose he didn't want rendered on canvas?"

Susanna laughed. "Interesting reference to Narcissus. Derek didn't make that connection. To him, this painting represents man's inability—or refusal—to self-reflect."

"Hmmm."

We stared at the image for a moment and then Susanna said, "Derek bought the print back in the fall. He spent a lot of time pondering its meaning. I haven't decided whether to leave it in here, hang it somewhere else in the house, or get rid of it."

"No rush to make a decision." I regarded the print for a few seconds more and turned my attention to the bookshelves. "You've made good progress."

"Yeah." Susanna surveyed her work. "It helps to keep moving." She pointed to the two remaining shelves of psychology books that needed to be packed and we got to work.

"So, you wanted to talk? Officer Brody told me this morning there haven't been any developments in the case." Susanna glanced at a few titles and then loaded the books in a box. "I doubt she's telling me the truth, though. I *am* a suspect." Her tone was matter-of-fact.

"I'll be blunt. Is there a reason for you to be a suspect?" I grabbed a few books off the shelf and placed them in the box. I didn't note the titles; my glance was on Susanna.

She smiled. "Am I on your suspect list too?" Her chuckle morphed into a sigh. "It comes with the territory, I suppose. The spouse is always the prime suspect, unless there's an ironclad alibi. I can't provide one." She crossed her arms and shifted her weight to one leg. "I know there's every reason to suspect me. All I can say is that I'm not having an affair. I'm not the beneficiary of a huge life insurance policy in Derek's name. Derek didn't physically abuse me. What other reasons could I have? Derek liked my cooking and I never nagged him about taking out the garbage. And he never left his socks or wet towels on the floor."

"Was Derek ever unfaithful?"

Susanna's eyes filled with tears.

"I'm sorry."

"It's okay" She wiped her eyes and dried her fingers with a swipe across her T-shirt. "The police have asked me. It's a logical query. It's just a shock every time it's asked." Susanna turned away, took a book off a shelf, and ran her finger along the book's spine. "Derek, to my knowledge, never had an affair. I can't be certain, of course, but I don't believe he was ever unfaithful to me."

I braced for Susanna's reaction to my next question. "Did Derek ever talk about his contentious relationship with Ashley Monico?"

Susanna shoulders drooped. "You know about that?"

I nodded. "Gretchen told me and Ashley filled in the details when she interviewed me the other day for a research project. I noticed in his bibliography on his Arden page that he was a co-author on more articles written by women than by men. I assume they were his students."

Susanna sank into the chair behind the desk. She put her elbow on the desk and rested her forehead against her palm. "Yes. He could be such a jerk. I knew he often took more credit than he deserved on his students' papers. I could never convince him that it was unfair and wrong. Derek thought his guidance counted for authorship. That without his oversight of the research, without his advising the student, the project would not have succeeded. He thought that he, the professional psychologist, made the biggest intellectual contribution." She wiped away a tear that glided down her cheek.

I realized Derek's treatment of his students was also an act of disloyalty toward Susanna. He spoiled the trust she had in him and of the principles she held. I moved to her side and patted her shoulder. "I'm sorry."

Susanna nodded, allowed herself one more moment of dejection, and then emerged from the gloom by scrambling to her feet and continuing the packing.

"Ashley must be on your suspect list." The three books she dropped into the box landed with a dull thud. "But I just can't believe she'd poison Derek. The problem had been resolved. Miranda would be her adviser soon and she had a promising future. In her career and with Kyle."

"Ashley attended your student barbecue. How was her mood? Did she and Derek interact?"

"Ashley was a lovely guest. She seemed to enjoy herself. She and Derek were cordial to each other. He gave her a warm welcome, but I didn't see them interact at all during the evening."

"And the others? Did everyone enjoy the evening?"

"Yes, I think so. Everyone was all smiles. Lots of laughing and happy chatter."

"Was Ashley the only student who spoke out against Derek's insistence for writing credit?" I glanced over the authors and titles before I stacked the books in the box. Derek had the writings of all the great minds of his field. Freud. Jung. Piaget. Skinner. Erikson. He also had texts by his contemporaries, names I didn't recognize. Seligman. Fredrickson. McTigue. Bronson. Marlucci. Taub.

"I've never heard that others spoke up about how Derek treated them. They were probably all too intimidated to fight for themselves." She stacked several books in the box. "I confess, I'm afraid to ask. I don't know if I want to know."

We worked in silence for a minute and then I asked, "Miranda deftly assumed leadership of the department. Did Derek ever mention that she was angling to succeed him?"

Susanna made a dismissive wave. "She wore him down with critiques and suggestions of how he ran the department. Miranda knows just how everything should be done. She probably already has a ten-page plan for department changes so it will operate at peak efficiency. Miranda also has a knack for knowing everything that goes on in the department, from the classroom to behind closed doors."

"A backstage gossip."

"They're everywhere," Susanna said with a tired laugh. Her expression turned determined. "Miranda would have the answer to your question. The one I don't want to ask. You've been kind to help me pack these books. Do you have time to pay a visit to campus and lend me some moral support?"

"Sure. Shall I drive?"

"No. I have a faculty sticker on my windshield. I can park anywhere."

Chapter Twenty

We headed to campus in Susanna's gray sedan. On the drive, she told me about her family and upbringing, her undergraduate and graduate years, and the early days of her and Derek's relationship. They'd met at a student string quartet concert a month into Susanna's first semester at Arden.

"There were no lightning bolts or Cupid's arrows," she said, laughing. "It was not love at first sight, but we knew at once we were simpatico. Our intellectual compatibility blossomed into friendship and then romance."

I gave a dry rejoinder. "The same with Mark and me. Our ability to share crayons at our kindergarten class's craft table showed we were meant to be one. It only took us forty-eight years to get together."

"Any regrets about the long delay? If you had gotten together earlier, you could've had a family."

"It worked out the way it was meant to happen." I hesitated, reluctant to ask if Susanna and Derek had wanted children. It's the most personal of questions and the answer is never my business.

"Lovely perspective."

We stopped at a traffic light; for a minute the only sound in the car was the ticking of the turn signal.

"Derek and I decided early on we wouldn't have children. We were consumed and satisfied in our careers. Our relationships with students have always been rewarding and fulfilled whatever need we had to nurture another human being and help them become an adult and contributing member of society. I've never regretted the decision, but this last week, a sorrow that we never had a child has mingled with my grief. Maybe I just selfishly want someone to share the loss with."

Susanna breezed past the outer lot where I'd parked a few days earlier and turned onto a two-lane road that circled the campus. In two minutes we pulled into a small parking area behind Hammes Hall.

She led the way into the building and up the stairs to the psychology department, stopping in the doorway of Bradley's office. "Hi, Bradley."

He looked up from his laptop's screen and registered surprise at our presence. "Susanna!" He sprang to his feet and greeted us. "Are you here to clear out Derek's office?"

"No. Just visiting."

"Well, it's good to see you. If you need help with anything, you know where to find me."

"There is something," Susanna said. She explained her project of packing Derek's books. "I'd like to donate them to the department. Will you recruit a couple of students to pick up the boxes?"

"Absolutely. Do you need help packing? I'd be glad—"

"No. With Veronica's help I've made good progress."

"All right. Just call me when you want the boxes taken away."

Susanna thanked him and we continued to Miranda's office, two doors down from Bradley's. She sat at her desk facing the window and the gorgeous cherry blossom tree that was in bloom outside it.

Miranda's welcome was effusive. She gave Susanna a lingering embrace, a kiss on both cheeks and asked Susanna how she was.

Susanna gave a perfunctory "I'm fine," and shut the office door. "I have questions and I want honest answers, Miranda." Susanna's authoritative tone impressed me. She had shed her figurative widow's weeds and donned a professional mantle.

I sat in the guest's chair in front of the floor-to-ceiling bookcase while Susanna claimed the seat next to the desk.

Miranda lowered the laptop's lid and folded her hands on her desk. Another professional suiting up. "Okay."

"First I'd like to know why you discouraged Ashley from filing a complaint against Derek. You should have allowed her to shine a light on the problem. Derek would've received a needed dose of humility."

"Ashley wanted to file a charge of harassment. Derek's behavior didn't rise to that level, and I didn't think her case against him would succeed. I believed it would have negative consequences for Ashley. I acted for her sake, not Derek's."

"I understand that. But if we continue to persuade young women to keep quiet for the sake of their careers, they will never enjoy those careers in full."

"I understand and agree," Miranda said. "In Ashley's unique case, I believed it better to keep the matter in the department and handle it by agreeing to be her adviser, starting next semester."

Susanna nodded. "What about Derek's other students? Did any of them have an issue with the guidance Derek gave them? Did he demean anyone else's work?"

"Not that I know of," Miranda said. "Ashley was the only person this past year who took public issue with Derek."

"*This* year?" Susanna asked

Miranda gave Susanna a contemplative glance. "There was a situation two years ago, during the fall semester." Miranda described an incident in which a female graduate student accused a male student of stealing her research idea. "Derek sided with the male student—"

Miranda's sudden silence gave me the impression she'd intended to say more. Perhaps complete the sentence with an "of course?"

"Is the female student still in the program?" Susanna asked.

"No. She graduated last May. There were other female students, over the past three or four years, who confided in me their disappointment and frustration with how Derek was advising them. He wasn't the supportive mentor they hoped—expected—him to be. I spoke with Derek about it on a few occasions."

"And he dismissed your concerns, as he did the students'?"

"Yes."

"And this behavior started just a few years ago? Derek wasn't like this when you joined the faculty?"

"No. It was fairly new. It began after—" Miranda lowered her gaze.

"I was awarded the Pulitzer."

Miranda nodded.

Susanna's questioning took a hairpin turn. "Did Derek ever sleep with a student?"

The blunt question left us in uncomfortable silence for a moment before Miranda gave a soft-spoken answer.

"Derek loved *you*, Susanna."

Susanna nodded, unable to speak.

I took up the conversation. "Did Derek have issues with anyone else in the department? Faculty or student, other than Ashley? Not minor disagreements but a matter that could affect someone's career?"

"No." Miranda picked up the square box of facial tissues on the far corner of her desk and moved it to within Susanna's reach. "Derek respected everyone in this department and at Arden."

Susanna pulled a tissue from the box and dabbed her eyes. "Thank you for your honesty, Miranda. I apologize for the interruption." She stood and tucked the tissue into her pocket. "I've been packing up Derek's home library and would like to donate them to the department. I just arranged with Bradley to have the boxes picked up."

"Thank you, Susanna." Miranda rose and rounded the desk. "Derek had an impressive collection of professional texts. I know his books will be treasured by all of us." She embraced Susanna. "Let's have lunch or dinner soon. Talk more pleasant subjects."

Susanna gave a vague nod and slipped into the corridor.

"Professor Rafferty!" Gretchen's outcry halted our progress to the stairwell. The post-graduate swept down the hall and engulfed Susanna in an embrace. "How are you?"

Susanna extricated herself from Gretchen's grip. "I'm fine, dear. Thank you for your lovely flowers and card. Your kind words were touching."

Noelle stepped from the pantry and stood in the middle of the hall, dunking a tea bag in a mug and watching the exchange between Susanna and Gretchen.

"I meant every word," Gretchen said, her earnestness palpable. "Derek was the best teacher I've ever had. I'm so fortunate that he was my mentor. I'm going to pass along everything I learned from him to every student I teach, starting in September."

"That's wonderful. Derek thought highly of you, Gretchen. He said you were an excellent student." Susanna signaled an end to the conversation with a turn toward the stairwell.

Gretchen's great mind didn't pick up the body language. "That means so much. Did you hear about the memorial we're planning for Derek? I'm leading the fundraising to buy a bench and tree that will be placed right outside the building. There'll be plaques, too, on the bench and by the tree. We'll hold a ceremony in mid-September. I hope you'll come."

"Of course I will. Send me the details."

Gretchen thwarted Susanna's attempted exit with another suffocating hug. "If there's anything I can do— anything at all!— please call me."

"I will, Gretchen. Thank you." With her firm but polite words, Susanna turned and resumed leading our departure.

I waved to Noelle and offered Gretchen a nod and followed.

We descended the stairs and left the building in silence. When we were outside, Susanna slipped on her sunglasses and blew out a frustrated breath. "Now I'm really deep into the anger stage of grief. I'm supposed to be furious at Derek for dying, but I'm livid at how he treated his female students. Because he was jealous of me! If I'd known he'd bullied other women and dismissed their work... Oh, I would've..."

Chapter Twenty-One

"Susanna never said what she'd have done," I told Carol an hour later. "Did she consciously stop herself from saying she'd have killed him or was she just so angry she got tongue-tied?"

"Maybe she'd have divorced him. What a jerk for being jealous of her success." Carol closed the door of her shop's refrigerator and adjusted her grip on the bucket of white roses she had taken from the case. "It would be interesting to know what Susanna does when you're not around." Carol led the way to her workroom.

"What do you mean?"

Carol set the bucket on the work table. We'd already carried in four other buckets of flowers from the refrigerator. She added the roses to the lineup and went over to a shelf and selected a vase from the more than two dozen she'd stocked in different sizes and shapes. "I mean is she pacing the floor, wracking her brain thinking of every person her husband knew who might have a motive to kill him? Or is she sipping cocktails on the deck, enjoying the fine weather and waiting for her next scene with the Emmy-winning Veronica Walsh?" Carol filled the vase with water from her double-wide sink.

"That's cynical, especially coming from you. I'd rather Susanna be consumed with grief than be a psychotic."

Carol shrugged and began arranging the flowers in the vase. "You and I both know that the wife, or the husband, is often the killer." She moved with speed and confidence in a performance that hypnotized me. My floral therapy isn't received only through my sense of smell but by sight too.

While she worked her magic I reflected on my busy afternoon.

"Maybe I shouldn't have mentioned Derek and Ashley's contentious relationship to Susanna."

"Why? I'll take off my cynic's cap. Let's assume she's innocent. Something you tell her might stir her memory and get information that will lead to the murderer."

"She moved fast to talk with Miranda to get the unvarnished truth about Derek. What if Susanna figures out who the killer is from what I tell her and confronts *that* person? The killer might get nervous and act again."

Carol cut the stems of several roses with a floral knife. Her quick moves made me cringe; in less adept hands, it wouldn't be the roses that lost a piece of themselves. "So stop sharing information with Susanna. Or even better, stop investigating. Leave the case to the police."

"Susanna asked me to help find Derek's killer."

"Well then, pal, you have a dilemma only the philosophy department can help you resolve."

"I don't know anyone in the philosophy department!"

"A psychologist would have a field day analyzing Derek's jealousy of his wife and transference of that jealousy onto his female students," I said to Mark on our post-dinner walk through my neighborhood. "You'd think Derek would be more self-aware."

"It's hard to be objective about your own relationships."

"Too close, I get it," I said. "Just as you historians need to wait a few years to properly evaluate a president's administration or a monumental event."

"You got it." Mark squeezed my hand. "Around again?"

"Sure."

We walked past my house and began our second walk around the block.

"What if Derek was in the way of something Miranda wanted? Maybe not the department chair but another position of power?

Would he have control over grant money for her research? Screw her by giving her a smaller share of the department budget? Could he have punished her for taking Ashley's side? Schedule all her classes at eight in the morning? Did I tell you what Dotsie called Miranda?"

Mark chuckled. "This should be good."

"She said Miranda was Derek's office wife who's morphed into a merry work widow."

Mark's chuckle became a full-throated laugh. "That would be a case study in opposites attract."

"What if they were involved? Opposites attract all the time."

"You mean conducting their own sleep research?"

I poked Mark's shoulder. "Be serious."

"If Miranda and Derek had a romantic relationship that soured, or a difficult professional relationship, then Miranda would have a motive to kill him."

"She certainly had the opportunity to poison Derek's soda."

We walked a short distance in companionable silence, my hand comfortable in Mark's and our strides in sync.

"I'm shocked by Derek's jealousy of Susanna's success," I said. "You'd think that an expert on human behavior would've recognized his own jealousy and done some self-improvement."

At the end of Willow Lane we stopped and talked with one of my neighbors for a few minutes. We strolled Primrose Drive, Birch Lane, and Sycamore Street back to Willow. When we neared my house, we were surprised by the presence of a blue Ford parked at the curb. The car's driver and passenger stood on my porch.

Kyle and Ashley.

"Do we have enough dessert for four?" Mark muttered.

"You really need to ask? You know I always have at least three packages of cookies and a box of Entenmann's cake in the kitchen cabinet."

"You're prepared for anything. A blizzard. Hurricane. Zombie apocalypse. Any cataclysm, you're ready."

"That's me. And now let's use my sweets supply to get some info out of this pair of PhDers."

We quickened our pace and met the couple midway up the driveway.

"We're sorry to show up like this." Kyle's expression was tight with worry. "I probably should've called first."

"That's all right." Mark gave the young man a congenial shoulder clap. "Join Veronica and me for dessert."

"We really shouldn't...we didn't mean to..." Kyle stammered.

"It's fine." I offered Kyle a smile and shared it with Mark. "We have plenty."

We trooped through the house. While Mark played host to the young couple at the backyard table, I bustled around the kitchen, making coffee and arranging on a plate a selection of cookies from my stash.

Though Ashley and Kyle each took a cookie, neither took a bite of the treat.

"Miranda told me about your and Susanna's visit this afternoon," Ashley said. "I had nothing to do with Derek's death. Neither did Kyle."

Kyle's dark eyes and tight expression conveyed his anxiety. "You know I was at the house a few days before Derek died. That means I had an opportunity to poison a beverage and then remove it later. And you know I had a motive." He and Ashley exchanged a glance. "I can't prove I didn't kill him. But I'm asking you, please, believe me."

"Kyle, I have no power over the case," I said. "I don't make the arrest or press the charge."

"But you've solved murders. You have tremendous influence with the police."

Ashley added, "You can tell them Kyle and I had no reason to kill Derek. I didn't do as I was told and swallow my feelings. I stood up for myself and for my work. Derek caused me a lot of anxiety, but it was all sorted out and the situation was resolved to my benefit. So I had no reason to poison Derek. It was a cruel act. I never wished Derek harm, even in my most furious moments."

Mark gave the students a reprieve from playing defense. "Kyle, does anything that happened at the party stand out in your mind? Did anyone spend an unusual amount of time in the house while everyone was outside? Anyone disappear for an unusually long period?"

Kyle's forehead creased in a display of deep thought. "I can't think of anything odd happening or of someone being away from the party for longer than it takes to go to the bathroom."

"Did you ever talk with Derek about how he treated Ashley?" I asked.

Kyle's face flushed. "I did."

I didn't expect that easy admission. Kyle is honest to a fault.

Ashley registered surprise and twisted on the bench to face him. "What? When?"

"At the party. I met him inside on my way to the bathroom. All I said was that I didn't like how he behaved and I was glad he wouldn't be your adviser for much longer. That's all I said," Kyle said with emphasis.

Except for the not-so-nice name you called him. Though Kyle didn't say the term of non-endearment to Derek's face. I couldn't blame Kyle for venting his anger. He cared for Ashley; perhaps he was in love with her.

"But later, I felt bad about saying it. I was a guest and was rude to Derek in his home. So on Monday, when I went to Hammes to meet Ashley for lunch, I stopped at Derek's office and apologized. He accepted, and we shook hands. He even said he admired me for defending Ashley." Kyle exhaled and his shoulders relaxed. "I'm so glad I spoke with Derek."

"I wish I'd cleared the air with Derek," Ashley said. "I didn't want to attend the party, but I did to show there were no *hard feelings.* But our relationship was still strained. I figured in time..."

Her regret lingered over a brief silence. We sipped coffee and nibbled on cookies.

"Ashley, were any other grad students irked by Derek's demand for writing credit?" I broke off a small piece from my second cookie and popped it into my mouth. "Did anyone come to you in private and complain?"

"No." Ashley shook her head. "Everyone else gave in to his demand."

"Someone could've held a grudge," Kyle said. "Maybe someone didn't like you how you were treated, but remained silent out of fear they'd be treated the same."

Ashley conceded his point. "True."

"Anyone angry about a poor grade," Mark asked, "or have a disagreement with Derek over their work?"

"Not that I'm aware," Ashley said.

I asked Kyle, "Have any of your peers had a problem with Susanna?"

Kyle shook his head. "No."

"You can be honest. I won't repeat anything you've said." Mark said with a kind glance.

Kyle bobbed his head. "I'm sure. All of Susanna's students love her. Everyone."

We talked about more pleasant subjects—mainly Kyle's and Ashley's PhD work—until our coffee mugs were empty and the cookies all consumed. Kyle dominated the conversation with a description of a permanent collection he was curating for the college.

"Letters exchanged between New York families and their loved ones serving at war time. We have letters dated from every conflict, from Afghanistan and Iraq all the way back to the 1700s. In fact, we just received the letters an Albany couple exchanged during the Revolution. Matthew Sullivan served in the first New York Regiment. The power of the messages isn't in what he describes about the battles, but his love for his wife and two children. I love the romance of history." Kyle dipped his head to hide his shy grin and blushing cheeks.

"Thanks for listening to us," Kyle said on the walk around the house to the front yard. Unclasping his hand from Ashley's, he extended his hand to Mark.

"Thank you for trusting us," Mark responded over their handshake.

We returned to the backyard and settled in the Adirondack chairs.

"*Do* we trust them?" I asked. "Were they telling the truth or engaging in a bit of reverse psychology? Telling us the truth but omitting one vital detail?"

"I believe Kyle," Mark said. "I can't see him poisoning Derek in an act of chivalrous revenge. He had the motive and opportunity and could easily obtain the means, but I just can't imagine Kyle's anger was strong enough to compel him to action. He's not a grudge-carrying type of person."

"Funny that you say *chivalrous*. I wonder what Ashley thinks of him playing knight in shining armor. I think she'd rather be her own hero. Kyle's quite the romantic, if turning red over love letters written in 1700s is any indication."

"Like I said, I doubt his romantic moves include poisoning insulting professors," Mark said.

"I hope not."

Mark reached across the armrests of his chair and mine and took my hand. "Let's end this talk for the night. Class dismissed."

"Will I get in trouble if I ask the professor to carry my books home?"

Mark grinned and leaned in for a kiss. Obviously not.

Chapter Twenty-Two

Round three of my interviews with my new pals from the psychology department took place on Friday. While waiting for Bradley to arrive, I wondered whether he, Miranda, and Ashley were comparing notes on me. Were their interviews more of an observation of my behavior than a gathering of data for their studies?

Bradley rang the doorbell at the stroke of one o'clock. He wore a short-sleeved cotton shirt in the shade of a light-blue sky, light-colored chino pants, and black loafers.

After he gave me profuse thanks for agreeing to the interview—"My profession would be in a shambles if people refused to talk with us"—we took our seats in the living room. He accepted a glass of ginger ale but declined my offer of cookies and pound cake, leaving the sweets until the end of our session.

Bradley began the interview with a summary of his project and then asked a few general questions about my life and career before delving into more probing queries.

"Was there ever a rumor about yourself that frightened you? A rumor you thought might end your career? Or do irreparable damage to your private life?" Bradley asked the question with such gentleness, his gray eyes, so full of compassion, that I believed he'd give me a therapy session right there in my living room if I'd answered in the affirmative. Hey, I was already on the couch.

My response, however, was no, but I didn't offer it immediately. I'd had my fair share of being the subject of rumors in my long career. Some gossip had originated on the *Days and Nights'* set, some had been spread by an industry person, and other rumors had been started by fans. If I were seen having lunch with a male co-star, there'd soon be whispers that we were having a torrid affair. If I had dinner with an actor or actress from one of the New York-based soaps, there would be chatter that I was going to leave *Days and Nights* for a plum role in another soap's cast. On top of all that was the constant gossip that my co-star Melanie Hughes and I hated each other, life imitating the fictional rivalry our characters had. We were too darn good at all those catfights we played.

I related this gossip history to Bradley. "The rumors never damaged my career, but I tired of having to explain over and over that I wasn't in love with my leading man, that I wasn't leaving the soap, and that Melanie was a close friend. I don't miss that part of my career at all. I can't imagine how much worse it is now. Rumors spread so much faster with all the social media sites."

"And yet the truth doesn't move so quickly. Some choose not to believe the truth. They prefer the salacious gossip and conspiracy theories. Rumors are based in jealousy and envy. They're weapons of revenge and the damage they do to human lives is tremendous."

"Has gossip affected your career?" I asked.

"I've fortunately never been the subject of rumors. At least nothing has reached my ears," Bradley added with a chuckle.

"That's good. Reputation is very important in the academic world."

Bradley agreed. "It can make or break a career."

"Did Derek have a good reputation among the faculty and students? Any unpleasant gossip whispered about him in the hallowed halls?"

Bradley rolled his pen between his fingers. "No gossip. And he had an excellent reputation. Being the department chair is a difficult job. It's a guarantee you'll upset someone at least once a day."

"It seems Derek upset the women of your department more than the men of your group."

"Derek wouldn't have been the first man to do that." At my

surprised reaction, Bradley hastened to add, "I certainly didn't approve of Derek's misogyny and bias. But I didn't have much power to do anything about it."

I get it. The junior members of the faculty keep their mouths shut about their misbehaving elders so they can secure their tenure, sweet class assignments, etcetera.

"Uh-huh. What was Derek and Miranda's relationship like?"

"Always professional." Bradley thumbed through the pages of his notebook.

Classic move! He's trying to turn the page on this conversation. I can be a psychologist too!

For a moment I imagined myself lecturing a roomful of college students on some brilliant psychological discovery I'd made. "Doctor Walsh" had a nice sound to it.

"Come on, Bradley." I adopted a teasing tone. "How many years have you studied human behavior? Nonverbal interactions that tell you what's going on in a person's head. The underlying meaning of their words. You haven't analyzed every single one of your colleagues and how they relate to each other?"

I'm getting so good at this.

Bradley chuckled. "You think I observe human behavior twenty-four/seven? Between us, staff meetings are so boring it's sometimes a struggle to stay awake. We don't talk psychology theory. It's all about budgets, schedules, and the agenda for the *next* meeting."

Humph.

I didn't display my frustration but kept a playful tone. "Sure. I bet you have a notebook full of observations of your colleagues that you're going to turn into an article or book and give a lecture about it. *The Psychology of Psychologists.*"

Bradley's laughter turned his complexion pink. "That's a great title. I might steal it."

"Better give me proper credit in the footnotes."

"Will do." Bradley closed the notebook and capped the pen. "Do you ever think of staging a comeback? If your agent called tomorrow and said you've been offered a role—"

"Been there, done that. I got that call a year ago and said no. And my agent's retired."

"You're lucky," Bradley said. "You've found happiness in a whole new career."

"A career in which no one gossips about me. That I know of."

"Well played. And I'm sure no one does. You're delightful. You're a two-time success story. A Barton legend."

"Once you're done with your research on gossip, you should do a study on how flattery gets you everywhere." I offered Bradley a plate of cookies and the soap-star smile I'd once deployed at photo shoots and on red carpets.

He laughed and took a cookie. "Both gossip and flattery have a powerful impact on self-esteem. It would be a fascinating combo to study." He went on to muse on how he would go about such a study.

I silently mused on my frustration. All the psychologists wanted to talk with me about my life experiences, but not one would utter a syllable about the murder of their fellow professor and friend. Are they all so exhausted from conducting professional research that they can't be bothered to pay attention to the happenings in their daily lives? Or do they each have a notebook filled with observations on their colleagues and will spill that gossip in career-building articles and books?

"Cookie for your thoughts?" Bradley asked, offering me the plate.

He bestowed on me a soap-star smile that made me wonder what Derek thought of his younger colleague. It happened on soaps: a young, not-surgically-enhanced gorgeous actor joins the cast and soon becomes the fan's favorite, wounding the egos of some older stars. Was Derek jealous of Bradley's youth, charm, handsome looks, and professional success? Derek could boast many achievements in his academic life, but Bradley's career promised to eclipse Derek's. Did Derek's healthy ego falter in Bradley's presence?

But then Bradley would be the dead man, killed by a colleague wild with envy.

Besides, Derek was Bradley's mentor who'd been guiding Bradley through the demanding tenure process. Like some of the mature soap stars—myself included—confronted with the new generation of actors, Derek put his ego aside and befriended his fellow academic for the good of his department and professional field. *Was it because Bradley was a man? Did Derek enjoy the spotlight Bradley's work shone on the department? Did he plan to claim some of it for himself in the years ahead, after Bradley earned tenure?*

I responded with a coy grin of my own. "Trying to bribe me with my own cookies?"

"Ha ha! I thought the cookies were a bribe to get me to write only wonderful things about you."

"Make me look smart and you can take the whole box home."

"I don't need to do anything to make you look smart, Veronica." Bradley's tone grew earnest. "It was a pleasure interviewing you. Thank you for your time and the generosity of your thoughtful answers."

"I'm a people-pleaser. What's the psychology term for that?"

"Why ruin the mood by saying you have a fear of rejection and Dependent Personality Disorder?"

"But you just did!"

Bradley laughed, I laughed, and he split a cookie in two and offered me one piece.

"And what about my need to solve crimes? Do I have a super-sized superego?"

Chapter Twenty-Three

"You professors speak well of each other when you're all alive and speak well of each other when one of you dies because it would be rude to speak ill of the dead. Do I make myself clear?"

"Crystal." Mark toasted me with his glass and took a deep sip of beer. "What's said in the ivory tower isn't repeated outside the ivory tower."

"Ha ha." I took a sip of my Seven and Seven, leaned back in my chair, and sighed. "So glad it's Friday."

"Ditto. A semester has never ended on such a dark note."

The silent minute that followed, in which we enjoyed our drinks, loving eye contact, and glances at the other civilized diners out to enjoy a pleasant evening at the Hearth, was shattered by a commotion in the entry from the hall.

Vicki's husband, Jordan, stood in the doorway, holding his younger son upside down by his ankles.

The boy twisted and flailed his arms. "No!"

The hostess, her expression set in a tense smile, squeezed past Jordan. She held several menus and started toward our table. Jordan followed and behind him came his eldest son, who slapped his father's butt with each step. Vicki pulled up the rear of the family parade, holding hands with her twin daughters. A shy Eliza walked with her gaze fixed on the floor while her sister stamped her feet, punched the air with her tiny fist, and shot a scowl at every diner she passed.

"Oh, no." My glance shifted to the unoccupied table next to ours. *No, no, no, no, no.*

Mark stole a look and then whispered, "Isn't that the family who lives next—"

"Yeah. The Shepards. And they're going to be our dinner neighbors!" My vision of enjoying the pizza Mark and I'd ordered faded to black.

"It's not too late to change our order to take-out."

"Hi, Veronica!" Vicki halted beside my chair and flashed a movie-star smile. "Nice to see you again!"

Her energetic cheerfulness begged the question: Was Vicki a preternaturally upbeat person or was she on some mood-enhancing substance? Was she a firm believer in the cliché that kids grow up so fast and she wouldn't let the fearsome foursome get her down or did she sneak a drink while her husband was strapping the kids into their car seats?

"Hey, Vicki. Hi, girls."

Eliza leaned against Vicki's leg and stole a quick look at me. Josie stuck out her tongue and blew a raspberry.

"She must keep you on your toes."

Vicki let out a giddy giggle. "And laughing, all day long."

Did she smoke something *or ingest* it *in a brownie?*

"Stop talk!" Josie punched Vicki's leg.

"Okay, Josie. Nice seeing you again, Veronica." Vicki threw a nod of acknowledgement to Mark and guided the tiny twosome to the table several feet from ours.

We watched the family settle around their table. The hostess and a server had set booster seats in two chairs, with, at the direction of Jordan, one empty seat between them. Vicki took that place between the girls.

Thank goodness. At least the dining room won't have to listen to Josie torture Eliza the whole evening.

With an amused look, Mark asked, "We're staying?"

"At the risk of heartburn or being hit by a plate of food, sure. Let's not allow the lively Shepards to ruin our evening."

Mark and I tipped our glasses together and took deeper than normal sips of our adult beverages.

The Shepards' server, already looking overwhelmed, handed menus to Vicki and Jordan.

Josie screamed and lunged for Vicki's menu. "Mine!"

Vicki gave the tot the menu and a kiss on her head.

I was not a mother, but I'd played one on *Days and Nights*, and so felt justified in clicking my tongue at the behavior. *If I had grabbed anything from my mother when I was that age, Mom would've slapped my hand and sent me to sit in the corner for a few minutes.*

Jordan sat across from Vicki and between their sons. He alternated between reading a menu and talking to each boy in turn. I did a double-take at the occupants of the table behind the Shepards' table.

Kyle studied a menu while Ashley kept her focus on the family. Her glance shifted and met mine. She nodded and looked down at the table. I thought she was looking at a menu and then realized she was writing on a notepad.

Our server set our appetizer—mozzarella sticks and marinara sauce to share—in the center of the table.

Mark nudged the platter toward me. "You first."

I leaned forward and whispered, "Ashley and Kyle are at the table right behind the Shepards." I selected a mozzarella stick.

Mark took a casual glance at the family and mouthed "hello" to Kyle.

"Ashley's observing the Shepards. She's been a busy bee scribbling her observations." I dipped the cheese stick in the sauce and popped it in my mouth.

"Interesting." Mark grabbed one of the sticks, dragged it through the sauce, and took a large bite.

I took another bite of my appetizer and savored its deliciousness. "I wonder how they paired up? Did Vicki approach—ambush, more likely—Ashley, or did Ashley think the twins great research subjects?"

"You're cynical this evening." Mark wiped a blob of sauce from his lips.

If only you knew what else I'm thinking. "Well, look at the evidence." I tilted my head in the Shepards' direction.

Mark's gaze followed and lingered on the family for thirty seconds. Tears streamed down Eliza's cheeks, Josie waved a spoon in a threatening manner, and the two boys banged their forks on the table while shouting, "We want food!"

"Are you sure you want to stay? We can take the pizza and run. A backyard twilight dinner would be nice."

I dismissed Mark's lovely suggestion. "We can have that any time. We have two tables of suspects right under our noses. Let's observe."

"What do you expect to observe?"

"I don't know. We have to watch the scene unfold."

Mark chuckled with amusement and swallowed a generous bite from the mozzarella stick.

"I wonder how they connected," I said.

"Maybe they met when Derek and Susanna had their grad students over for dinner," Mark said.

"Maybe the girls crashed the party the way they stomped into the barbecue and Susanna introduced the students to Vicki. That gave Vicki the idea to approach one of the students with her proposal, and she landed on Ashley. If Vicki mentioned that Derek didn't want to conduct the study, Ashley may have seen it as a way to prove him wrong. Succeed where he assumed failure. An excellent way to get back at Derek for the misery he caused her."

"A much better way than poisoning him," Mark said.

"Right. Ashley would want Derek to see her succeed and know that he had no part in it. No credit for him!"

I glanced at the family. The server was taking their order; all the kids clamored for soda. Vicki showed some maternal mettle. "No. You will all have milk with dinner."

A pout went around the table like the wave at a football game, and Josie punched Vicki's arm.

Vicki covered Josie's hand with hers. "No hitting."

With her free hand Josie swung and connected with Vicki's jaw. Vicki didn't acknowledge the glancing blow.

"Who knew this was going to be Fight Night at the Hearth?" Mark asked, amused. "Why don't you go over and ask Ashley how she came to be the family's psychologist?"

"And leave you with all the mozzarella sticks? I don't think so, buddy." For show I took another cheese treat from the platter. "I wonder if Miranda knows that Ashley is doing this."

"She might. Remember she said at the party that the family was 'ripe with possibility,' "

"That's right!" I leaned forward, my shoulders hunched over my plate, and spoke *sotto voce*. "Miranda may be leading the study on the Shepards and Ashley is collecting the data!"

"If that's the case, I hope Miranda is paying for Ashley's and Kyle's meals." Mark raised his glass of beer to his lips.

We ate in silence for a minute. Mark gazed out the window to the activity along Orchard Street, and I enjoyed tastes of our appetizer while stealing glances at the family of six.

Derek said that he looked forward to seeing what the kids were like in fifteen years' time.

My imagination took a trip to the future. The twins would be in high school. I pictured Eliza a straight-A student and teacher's pet. Sweetest in the class. Josie would be the class mean girl, head of some exclusive clique. *She'd probably shut her sister out of the group.* Kids would tease that Josie was Eliza's "evil twin."

Stop your cynicism. You're stereotyping two toddlers who haven't learned boundaries or mastered self-control.

"Where are you?" Mark had stopped watching people out on

Orchard and moved his studious attention to me. "You look very far away."

"I am. The late twenty-thirties." I admitted to a daydream of Josie and Eliza in their teen years.

"Mine!"

Josie's cry drew our attention back to our dining neighbors. Perched on her knees and with her belly resting on the table, she stretched her arms toward the appetizer platter that was inches out of her reach.

Mark snickered. "I bet her parents would love to instantly age their kids past the *terrible two* years."

"We soap folks are expert at that. We aged children from two years of age to seven to eighteen like that." I snapped my fingers. "There's even a name for it. *Soap Opera Rapid Aging Syndrome.*"

My interest in the Shepards waned and, when our pizza arrived, Mark and I dug in with gusto and gave our attention to the meal and each other. Though there were several squeals from the kids and utensils were thrown on the floor several times, but once the food came, peace reigned at the family's table. Vicki gave a strong maternal performance; she was attentive to her children's every need and doled out praise for the smallest action: her eldest son's chewing with his mouth closed, her youngest son's taking off his baseball cap at the table, and Josie's cessation of kicking her legs against her chair.

When they finished their meal, she promised the kids they'd stop for ice cream on the way home as a reward for their excellent table manners.

"Do I get ice cream too?" Mark asked.

"With whipped cream and two cherries. But let's hang around. We might be able to talk with Ashley and Kyle and find out how they came to be the Shepards' *dining companions* for the evening."

The family left, with Vicki pausing at the young couple's table for a moment to speak with Ashley. Ashley gave her a smile and gestured to her notepad.

I guess Ashley's got a lot of material for her study. Or maybe she pretended to be taking notes and instead wrote a guide to her future self on how not to raise her own child.

A few diners traded relieved smiles when the last Shepard disappeared into the hall, and the older man sitting behind me said to his wife, "They shouldn't allow children under five in here."

His wife chastised him with a sharp "This is a family restaurant," and I silently scolded myself. *There'd be something wrong if kids didn't push boundaries. Josie will probably grow up and discover a cure for every horrible disease. Eliza will learn how to manage her sister and end up the president who brings everlasting peace to the world.*

Kyle gave a tiny jerk of his head toward our table and he and Ashley came over and said hello.

"Looks like you had a working dinner." I offered Ashley a smile of commiseration.

She laughed. "Yeah. Thank goodness I was able to sit with Kyle and not the family."

"I think Ashley should volunteer a few evenings of babysitting to get deeper into her research," Kyle said. He winked and squeezed Ashley's shoulder.

"How did you end up with the assignment? Derek was adamant he wasn't going to include the family in a research study."

"Vicki called Miranda a couple of days ago. She said that Derek had shown interest in observing the girls, because they're twins, and asked Miranda if she wanted to take on the study."

"Wow." I stole a glance at Mark, who appeared equally surprised. *Did Vicki really believe Derek wanted to include her kids in a study or did she knowingly lie to Miranda?* "Obviously Miranda was interested."

"Miranda hasn't committed. She suggested I observe the family and see if there is anything new we can contribute to twin research. I thought it would be better to observe them without the kids knowing they were being watched."

"Observing them in their natural habitat," I cracked.

That elicited snickers from Kyle and Mark, who asked, "Have you come to a conclusion?"

"There's been *a lot* of research on twins. I didn't see anything tonight that would bring something unique to the literature."

"Have you watched Vicki's videos?"

Ashley rolled her eyes. "Yeah. They're more instructional videos on how not to parent."

"What are you going to tell Miranda?" I asked.

"That we should give Vicki a polite but hard pass."

"Miranda should change her number after that phone call." We laughed at Mark's remark. "I don't think Vicki will be happy."

"Oh well," Ashley said. "I'm not giving another minute to observing those kids. I have enough on my plate."

"Now you can put your notebook away and enjoy dessert in peace," Mark said.

Kyle groaned. "We thought we'd stop for ice cream."

"Vicki will get the wrong idea if you show up right behind them," I said. "She'll think you're still observing them and entertain daydreams of her kids gaining worldwide fame. To be on the safe side, I think you should drive over to Bear Lake for ice cream. You can window shop in all the quaint shops and enjoy your ice cream in peace."

Kyle and Ashley exchanged a thoughtful look.

"That might be nice." Ashley's eyes sparkled with romance. "We can skip the window shopping and sit by the lake and watch the stars come out."

Kyle took her hand and they interlaced their fingers. "Thanks for the idea, Veronica."

"Young love." I sighed and watched the couple return to their table. "Want to drive to Bear Lake for ice cream? We'd have to find another place to sit, or they'd think we were following them."

"I'd rather sit in your backyard and watch the stars come out with my favorite star beside me."

"That's smooth. You're lucky I'm a cheap date."

We lingered at our table for a few more minutes. Ashley and Kyle paid their bill and departed for the ice cream by the lake portion of their evening and Mark and I digested our meal and what we'd just learned.

"So is Miranda wise for giving the Shepards an audition for a role in a research study?"

Mark smirked. "Vicki did put on a bit of a performance, didn't she?"

"Rather hammy." I chomped on a cold chunk of pizza crust left on my plate and followed it with a swallow of soda.

"Miranda may have agreed just to get rid of Vicki, once and for all," Mark said. "She gave the raucous family an hour of observation, albeit done by a psychologist-in-training."

"I doubt Vicki noted that distinction. Attention is attention."

"You're right about that. Vicki's desperate for attention, more for herself than her children, I think. She wants validation for her parenting skills more than she wants her children to be acknowledged for their specialness. That's my two cents."

"That's quite insightful," I said.

Mark offered me a pleased grin. "Historians engage in a bit of psychology, too, on the subjects we study."

"Maybe you should write the book on the Shepards."

"No, thanks. I'd lose my historian street cred."

We paid the bill and enjoyed the short walk from the Hearth to my house. By the time we'd settled in the backyard with bowls filled with scoops of chocolate ice cream, the stars were indeed taking the stage for a sparkling performance.

Chapter Twenty-Four

Mark's observation of Vicki and her need for attention hovered in my thoughts when I climbed into bed and was still on my mind the next morning when I walked to All Things. His assessment that Vicki wanted approval for her parenting skills may've been correct, but I wondered if there was another validation that needed fulfilling.

I may've dismissed my suspicion too soon.

I did a couple of hours work at the shop and at eleven headed up Orchard Street to Carol's shop.

"I'm about to head over to Saint Augustine's to set up for a wedding. Want to come?"

"Are you going to put me to work?"

"Of course. Think of it as payment for all the floral therapy I've given you."

"I didn't know I was running a tab."

I got a massive therapeutic dose of flower power on the way to the church. The back of Carol's delivery van was packed with blooms in the bride's color theme of lavender and white.

"I might pass out from the abundance of scent before we get to the church."

With a flourish of her finger, Carol opened the passenger window. "Stick your head out the window and take deep breaths." She turned out of the alley behind her shop and onto Pine Street. At the traffic light Carol made a right onto Orchard Street. "So is your visit social or related to the murder case?"

"The case. Mark and I went to the Hearth for dinner last night and were treated to a performance." I told Carol about the Shepards and Ashley.

"Kyle's a good boyfriend for sitting through a meal with Ashley's attention on the next table."

"Maybe she'll return the favor and spend an hour in the library watching him read up on the War of 1812."

"True love." Carol made a left turn onto Maple Lane.

"Are they so in love that Kyle poisoned Derek for how he treated Ashley? He has a strong romantic streak." I told Carol about Kyle's waxing poetic about the collection of wartime love letters he's curating. "He's a sweet guy and he readily admitted to confronting Derek at the party. And then he confessed that he was at Hammes Hall on Monday! He said he went there to meet Ashley for a lunch date and took the opportunity to apologize to Derek for his behavior. I know I'm cynical, but how convenient. He put himself right at the scene of the crime."

"Sometimes a cigar is just a cigar."

"Ugh!" I ignored Carol's laughter and glanced out the window. "But I digress. Mark theorized that what Vicki really wants is attention for her parenting skills rather than for her children."

"She wouldn't be the first."

"He may be right," I said, "but I wonder if what she's starved for is attention for who she is besides being a mother. She's only *Mommy* to four kids. She's *Vicki* to many more people."

Carol slowed to a stop at the junction of Maple and First Street. "Why would she press for her children to be the subject of a research paper if she wanted to be the center of attention?"

"Maybe she used the kids to get Derek's attention."

"You think she was in love with Derek?"

We arrived at our parish church of Saint Augustine. Carol turned into the lot and backed the van into a parking spot near the church's main entrance.

"Yeah. Or at least she's in love with the life she sees next door.

Derek and Susanna lived a peaceful, intellectual existence. I imagine them out on their deck in the evening, discussing their day. Smart talk about their work."

"A classic case of the grass was greener in the professors' yard."

"Yes. Vicki has four kids and a husband to take care of, plus a big house to keep in order. She does work at the village hall, but I bet she doesn't have much *adult* conversation. It's all 'go in the potty' and 'eat your green beans' and 'don't beat your sister with the wiffle ball bat.' "

"I can understand all that. Can you prop open the doors?" Carol jutted her chin toward the heavy wooden doors that opened into the church vestibule.

"Sure."

While Carol opened the van's rear doors, I trotted to the church and pushed hard on three sets of double doors so they'd stay open for us to breeze through from the entrance to the altar, our arms laden with the floral arrangements.

"And you think Vicki killed Derek because he didn't reciprocate her feelings for him? A case of unrequited love?" Carol handed me a white plastic vase that overflowed with white and lavender roses and fragrant lilac sprigs. "Can you carry two?"

"I can. Do you trust me is the question?"

Carol gave me a side-eye look. "I think so." She placed a second arrangement in the crook of my left arm, making sure I had a tight grip on it before she let go.

She scooped up two more arrangements and we walked down the cement sidewalk and across the wide brick area to the church door.

"Vicki may've transferred her need for attention as a woman into a desire for validation as a mother. When Derek showed disapproval for her maternal methods and the videos she's made of her children, she took it for a rejection of her whole identity."

"That's quite a psychological workup you've done." Carol

stopped in the vestibule between the outer and inner doors. "Vicki's probably like a lot of moms of young kids. She doesn't feel attractive, she's tired all the time, and, like you said, her conversations aren't intellectually stimulating. Maybe she did seek affirmation from Derek because her husband isn't giving it to her right now and maybe she snapped and gave Derek a glass of something mixed with antifreeze. And maybe she didn't." She adjusted her grip on one of the arrangements. "Let's have good thoughts now and go set up for this wedding."

"Good idea. I don't want to bring negative energy down on the bride and groom. And divine wrath on me for thinking the worst of Vicki."

I followed Carol into the entrance hall and church nave. At her direction, I placed the two arrangements on the floor before the altar. She set her arrangements behind the altar, on pedestals to each side of the chairs where the priest and deacon sit.

I fussed over the position of the arrangements for a minute and then turned to move up the aisle to assess the vases' placement. A man and a woman stood against the back wall, several feet from the two rooms where the parish priests heard confessions every Saturday between eleven and noon. I didn't know the man. My first glimpse of the woman sent a chill through me.

Vicki was first in line to unburden her sins.

We exchanged half-waves of recognition. She bent her head in reflection, and I turned my attention back to the flowers.

Lovely. The bride chose well, and Carol did her usual excellent work.

Carol joined me and glanced over the altar. "Looks good." She paused. "I love church weddings, but not many couples are having them these days. They're getting married at the reception site or having destination weddings."

We went out to the van and carried into the church two long boxes filled with tulle-and-flower decorations for the pew ends.

Carol took the section to the right of the center aisle, and I worked on the left section, placing a decoration over the curved back of each pew. The pieces were beautiful—a large white rose with a sprig of lilac on each side, wrapped in white tulle with tails that dangled a few inches and stems of myrtle adding a pop of green.

While Carol and I were outside, Vicki had gone into the confessional. I'd decorated half the pews when she exited the room and knelt in the last pew in the section next to where I worked. She kept her head bowed in prayer and dabbed her eyes a couple of times with a tissue.

Don't blow this out of proportion and make wild assumptions. She could've confessed anything. She can be upset about anything. Or she may not be upset at all, but filled with gratitude and grace.

Carol and I finished and stood by the baptismal font at the back of the nave. We admired our handiwork for a minute.

"Beautiful work, pal. You're so talented." I put my arm around Carol's shoulder and squeezed it.

"Thank you. Thanks for helping. It's fun having you along."

We took one last look and went out to the van. I was buckling my seatbelt when Vicki dashed out of the church. Without a glance in our direction, she hurried into the SUV parked three spots from the van.

"What's on your schedule for the rest of the day?" I asked.

"I'll come back here later to remove the pew decorations. Otherwise, I'll be at the shop."

"What will you do with the flowers?"

"The bride's sister will pick them up on Monday. I think they're going to distribute them among the wedding party and the bride's and groom's mothers."

"A sweet reminder of the day."

"Yeah. What's your plan for the afternoon?"

"Food shopping. House cleaning. Spend some time at All Things."

"Who would've ever thought that you and I would end up owning businesses a stone's throw from each other?" Carol shifted into *Reverse* and backed the van from the curb.

"I didn't." I waited for the maneuver to be complete and the van headed toward Maple Lane. "It was always obvious that you would have a floral empire, but soaps were hot when I landed on *Days and Nights.* I thought I'd be there forever."

"No regrets, right?" Carol's glance for oncoming traffic landed on me for a beat.

"None. I love being your business neighbor."

Carol flashed a pleased grin and turned onto Maple.

I had no regrets about how my life's course had run. My acting career had made me happy, and I was devastated when the soap was canceled. But I soon had the opportunity to buy All Things. The decision to take over the boutique had launched me into the most fulfilling phase of my life.

Can Vicki say the same? Is her life what she'd hoped it would be? Was there fulfillment in her days or only hours of frustration and fatigue?

My thoughts went back to Derek's refusal to give Vicki's children the attention she wanted for them. Did his rejection trigger her?

Carol and I chatted on the short drive back to Orchard Street. She turned into the alley behind her shop and parked outside her stockroom's door.

"Do you want me to help you remove the pew decorations?" I unbuckled my belt and slid from the van.

"Thanks, but no need. It'll take me just a couple of minutes to pack them up."

We passed through the stockroom and into the larger work room. The voice of Amy, Carol's assistant, through the open doorway to the front of the shop. "How about a basket?"

"They're all so beautiful! Yes, I think a basket will cheer up my friend."

Is that...?

I followed Carol into the shop, where Amy and Vicki stood near the refrigerator case.

"Hi, ladies," Amy said.

Vicki gave us a bright smile. Gone from her expression were all traces of tears, sorrow, guilt, regret, or whatever she felt in the church pew. "Hi, Veronica. Seeing you set up the beautiful flowers at the church inspired me. I thought I'd bring Susanna a fresh bouquet. I'm sure the condolence flowers are drooping and have lost their petals by now."

"That's a lovely idea," I said.

Vicki turned away, giving her attention back to the selection of floral arrangements in the refrigerator. I glanced at Carol. She acknowledged me with an arch of her brow and walked behind the counter.

"I think I'll take that one."

The refrigerator door swooshed open and closed and Amy, carrying a basket filled with various yellow and white flowers, led Vicki to the counter.

Vicki pulled a credit card from her wallet and tapped it on the payment terminal. "Derek's colleague Professor Liu is interested in studying the twins. Her research assistant was seated at the table next to ours last night at the Hearth."

"That's exciting." I had a jab of pity for Vicki. Miranda's *interest* had shot her hopes sky high; soon the balloon would be punctured and Vicki would fall back to earth.

Will she get the message and allow her kids to have an unexamined childhood or would she ring up Bradley or Tony next and make her pitch?

"Veronica, do you have time for coffee?" Vicki tucked the credit card back in her wallet.

Surprised, I blurted "I do." A flash of heat filled my cheeks.

"Listen to me. I spend twenty minutes setting up for a wedding, and now I think I'm the bride. Coffee would be great."

We bought our beverages at the deli and sat on a bench outside the antique shop, the flower basket between us.

I admired them and said, "It's thoughtful to buy these for Susanna. She'll be delighted."

Vicki blew on her coffee to cool it before taking a sip. "I figure now that the memorial service is past and everyone's given their condolences, people will get on with their lives and forget that Susanna's still grieving. I feel so bad that she's all alone in that big house."

Vicki is thoughtful. Or are the flowers a part of her penance? I chided myself for my cynicism. "Susanna's blessed to have such a kind neighbor."

She took a second deep sip of coffee. "I've wanted to ask you something since I saw you at Susanna and Derek's barbecue."

Oh, boy. Has she moved on from wanting her children to be the focus of a psychologist's study to desiring a larger audience for the kids? Or does she want me to appear in her videos with her rambunctious foursome? Nanny Veronica?

"When the girls were born, I really wanted to sign them up for modeling and acting jobs, but my husband convinced me to wait."

"Wise decision. You've had their adorableness all to yourself. Running around to photo shoots and spending hours on sets would make you even more exhausted than you are."

"Yeah." Vicki watched cars go by on Orchard Street for a few seconds. "I met with a talent agent a couple of months ago. She thought the twins were cute but not right for acting gigs."

I bit my tongue and imagined the scene in the agent's office. Josie obstreperous, Eliza wailing. "It's more demanding than you think."

"The agent mentioned temperament."

"Yeah. Long hours. Strangers—"

"I really believe Josie and Eliza would do well. You know, like those twins on the sitcom back in the nineties. I was wondering... You know casting people."

"Only the *Days and Nights* casting director. She retired when the show was canceled."

"Is there anyone else you know who might give the girls an opportunity?"

Good grief. First I have Derek's professor pals mining the depths of my psyche about my career and now his neighbor wants to take advantage of my acting connections to get her kids into show business.

My first sip of coffee burnt my tongue. "Ooh, hot!" I blew a few puffs to simultaneously cool my mouth and coffee. "Vicki, may I ask why you're so eager for your children to be noticed? First you want them to be the focus of psychological research and now you want Josie and Eliza to be actors and models."

Vicki put on a patronizing grin. "They're *so* special! Josie and Eliza do the most remarkable things every day. Of course my sons are special too. But the girls, because they're twins, have this indescribable connection. It's otherworldly." Vicki's cornflower blue eyes glistened with pride. "It's like they were one body split into two. Sometimes it's spooky how alike they are. They have their own language. Verbal and nonverbal! Once in a while, I catch them exchanging a look. They're communicating without speaking!"

She continued her rhapsodic monologue on the wonders of her twins. On the *Days and Nights* set I'd witnessed the special bond twins share in the relationships between the boys or girls who portrayed my and other characters' children. The bond was unusual and could be an extraordinary force to witness. But...

How do I gently tell Vicki that though her children are special, their bond isn't super extraordinary in the world of twins? I took a sip of coffee. *You don't have to burst that balloon. Just tell her.*

"I'm sorry, Vicki, but most of my contacts in the soap world are retired or I haven't kept in touch with them. I think the agent gave you good advice. You should wait a few years. When the girls have matured, they'll be able to choose whether they want to act. The lifestyle is hard for kids."

Vicki's frown deepened.

"Your children will grow up fast. You should enjoy the exclusive time you have with them now."

"I do." Vicki gazed at the shops across the street. With a move of her glance back to me, she changed the conversation. "The night Susanna and Derek had the party for their graduate students, I saw Derek and one of the students talking at the end of the driveway, and it didn't seem like lighthearted party chatter. Derek had a serious look and it looked like the student was crying. Not loud, but she did wipe her eyes a few times."

"How far were you—"

"I was at the bathroom window upstairs. I was bathing the girls."

"Who was the student?"

"Umm... I don't know her name. She has blond hair that she had in a braid."

Gretchen!

"You know who I'm talking about?" Vicki's gaze grew keen.

"Yes."

Vicki was silent for a few seconds; I wondered whether she was waiting for me to identify Gretchen. "I felt bad for her. I though Derek might've told her she'd failed a class or he gave her upsetting news about her dissertation or something."

"Hmmm... yeah. I have no idea."

"Derek went back to the party and she stood in the driveway for a couple more minutes. Pulling herself together, I suppose."

I felt sorry for Gretchen too, if Vicki's assumption was true. "Perhaps it was nothing."

"Maybe. I could be wrong. I'd forgotten all about it until last night and thought you should know." Vicki enjoyed a whiff of the flowers' scent. "It's a puzzle, isn't it? Who would poison Derek? What if the police never figure out who did it?"

"I have confidence they will."

"For Susanna's peace of mind, I hope they do. And speaking of Susanna, I should get these flowers to her. Nice seeing you again, Veronica. Thanks for the show biz advice."

I hope you follow it. "You're welcome."

Vicki walked away with a spring in her step and a swing of the arm carrying the basket.

Had Vicki's confession at the church lightened her spirit? Or had telling me of Derek and Gretchen's conversation—an allegedly upsetting talk—given her a shot of civic pride?

Or was it a diversion?

Chapter Twenty-Five

"I'm suspicious of the timing of Vicki's report," I said to Mark that evening. "She's too sharp to have *forgotten all about it* until last night."

"I can guess what your new theory is. Vicki first asked Gretchen to write an article on the twins, but Gretchen refused and Vicki's offended?"

"Correct, Professor Burke. You're so smart." I raised my glass in salute.

"Do you think Vicki is lying about seeing Gretchen and Derek?"

"No. She would be the one in need of psychological study if she fabricated the whole thing. Or in need of a thorough examination by an ophthalmologist. She may've misinterpreted what she saw."

"Along the lines of Gretchen had a speck of dust or a lash in her eye and wasn't crying?"

"Yeah. There's some distance between Vicki's house and the end of Derek's driveway. Far enough that Vicki couldn't hear them. Gretchen wasn't wailing for the whole neighborhood to hear. But if she was crying, what could Derek have said to cause the tears?"

"I think you have a theory on that too." Mark gave me a look and took a sip of his soda.

"Derek ended their romantic relationship."

"That's a doozy. You should've been a soap opera writer."

"There's still time. Maybe I'll whip together a few scripts in my spare time. Create a new soap."

'Revive the genre.'

"I think I'll set it at a college in northern New York. Hmmm..." I made an exaggerated show of thinking. "Maybe Arden will allow us to film on campus."

"I'm sorry I made the suggestion."

"I wonder what Vicki was sorry for in the confessional."

"Don't go there."

"You're right." I took a swig of my drink. "If Derek did upset Gretchen, she either got over it or she's a terrific actress. She acts as if Derek hung the moon. What academic matter could've gotten her in a twist?"

"It could be any number of things. Derek gave Gretchen constructive criticism about her work that she took the wrong way. A paper she wrote was rejected by a prestigious journal. She didn't get a grant or award she applied for. Vicki could've misinterpreted a simple case of disappointment. It would be odd, though, for Derek to deliver academic news at the party."

"He would be a party pooper at his own party."

Mark chuckled. "I think even Derek would've had the grace to break bad news at a quieter time and in a more private place."

Unless the eager Gretchen pressed Derek for an answer. *To what question, though?*

"What grants and awards would Gretchen apply for?" I asked Mark after dinner.

"There are a few prizes Arden awards PhD students. The Arden Instructor Prize is given to four or five doctoral candidates to teach an undergraduate course they've designed. Each winner is awarded an eight-thousand-dollar stipend. It's a terrific opportunity for professional development."

"That prize must look great on a C.V. for a person with a PhD hot off the press."

"It does. There are several other grants and fellowships doctoral candidates entering their dissertation defense year can win. The top amount given is five thousand dollars."

"Gretchen is going into her defense year. Have the awards been announced?"

"Yeah. A week or two ago." Mark tapped on his phone's screen. "Let's see." He was quiet for several seconds, intent on his search for the announcement releases. "Here we go. Raymond Cabrera of the psychology department is one of the five winners of the Instructor Prize." Mark read the description of Raymond's proposed course.

"That went in one ear and out the other," I said of the class Raymond had designed on behavioral analysis. "Did anyone from your department win?"

"A couple of our folks won stipends, but the other four Instructor prizes went to doctoral candidates from Sociology, Economics, Political Science, and Philosophy."

"What about the other awards? Did Gretchen or anyone else from the psychology department win?"

Mark read aloud the press release announcing the winners of the several grants available for doctoral candidates. Gretchen had been awarded a three-thousand-dollar stipend for her ongoing research.

"Good for her," I said, "but a disappointment if she'd applied for the Instructor Prize. She must have, if her goal is to join the Arden faculty."

I recalled Dotsie's theory that Gretchen had chosen her own interests when she'd sided with Derek against Ashley. *Gretchen didn't risk her own academic achievement by angering the department chair. But she didn't win the award, and she may blame Derek for that.*

"Not winning doesn't end her dream. Or make it harder to achieve," Mark said.

"True." *But for a Type-A overachiever like Gretchen...* "On what day were the announcements made?"

Mark returned to the announcement posts. "Two weeks ago, yesterday—"

"Friday. Which was the day after Susanna and Derek's party for their students."

I sympathized with Gretchen. I'd been blessed with several Emmy nominations in my long career, but had won only once. I always got over the disappointment, but the sting of not winning had lingered for some fellow actors and turned into bitterness.

"Do advisers have a say in who gets an award?" I asked.

"We give recommendations. If more than one doctoral student from a department applies for the Instructor Prize, the chairperson ranks the applications according to the department's course needs."

"So, if the department already has a course on the schedule that's similar to one an applicant has designed, the chairperson would give that application a low rank?"

"Correct."

"Sounds like an opportunity for a professor who might have a favorite—"

Mark interrupted with a sigh. "This must be the one hundred-and-seventh time I've had to remind you that real life isn't like the soaps."

"I'm a terrible student. I need private tutoring, Professor." I bat my eyelashes and leaned over for a kiss.

"Our private *tutoring* sessions aside," Mark said after our lips had parted, "we professors have high expectations for our students. We don't play favorites. Academic excellence is always the number one criterion for ranking and awarding students."

"I know you wouldn't allow your personal opinion of a student to cloud your assessment of their academic qualifications, but I bet other professors do."

"All right. I concede. It does happen that a person, in any profession, allows personal feelings to influence their professional judgement. I'm sure soap writers have given favored actors juicy storylines while the less popular actors get one or two scenes a week."

"The people you really don't want to offend are the makeup and wardrobe folks," I said. The stories I could tell of actors looking like a hot mess after being rude to Heather or Sharon. I always made sure I got along with everyone."

"Beloved by all." Mark took a turn at displaying affection and we shared a lingering kiss.

Derek, however, was not beloved by all.

Chapter Twenty-Six

Mark and I took a day off from our work and cares and spent Sunday at the Franklin D. Roosevelt Presidential Library and Museum in Hyde Park in Dutchess County. Though it was a two-hour drive from Barton, we enjoyed the scenic route, which included the crossing of the Hudson River, and stopped on the way home for dinner at a lovely Italian restaurant that overlooked Lake George.

At ten o'clock Monday morning I made a beverage run to the bakery. Gretchen and Bradley sat at a window table next to the door.

What's this off-campus meeting all about? Could they be...?

My response of "Good morning, my psyche-studying friends!" to their enthusiastic greeting elicited laughs and an invitation from Bradley to join them.

I gave Anita Rizzuto the staff's orders—a mix of cups of hot coffee and an iced version of the beverage—and plopped into the chair Bradley had pulled over from an unoccupied table. In a confidential whisper I asked, "Are you two observing Bartonites for some groundbreaking study?"

Bradley leaned forward and in a low voice answered, "No."

"I'm very disappointed."

He grinned. "We are talking current and future research projects. Gretchen is catching me up to speed on the work she did under Derek's guidance. I thought it would be more enjoyable if we talked in a relaxed setting rather than in my office or the campus cafeteria. "

And they had to come to Barton to find a relaxed setting? Don't want to meet anyone they know from Arden?

"The coffee is definitely better here than Arden's cafeteria." Gretchen raised her cup to emphasize her point. "Not to mention everything in the display case."

"Don't I know it." I bestowed a red-carpet smile on her. "Congratulations on the stipend you were awarded. Mark showed me the press release the other night."

"Thanks. Every *little* bit helps." Gretchen sounded more enthusiastic about the baked goods in Rizzuto's display case than in her academic achievement.

I ignored the emphasis on the amount of the stipend and continued to praise Arden's psychology team. "And a fellow psychology PhD candidate won one of the Instructor Prizes. That's very prestigious. I'm sure these successes boost the department's profile and make you more attractive to potential undergrad and graduate students."

"We're working hard to be one of the leading programs in the nation." Bradley tilted his head back to finish his coffee.

"I understand Derek's recommendation would've been instrumental to his students winning the awards." I landed an innocent gaze on Gretchen.

She trained her attention on her half-eaten chocolate-glazed donut. She split the half in half and popped it in her mouth. Mmhmm."

Bradley said, "Derek will be remembered for his advocacy of the students and faculty. We're going to institute the Derek Morley Award next year. It will be a financial award given to both an exceptional undergraduate in the department and an outstanding graduate student."

Anita brought my order arranged in a cardboard box. I thanked her and set the box in the center of the table.

"You attended the party Derek and Susanna had for their grad students, right?" I asked Gretchen.

She hesitated before saying, "Yeah, I was there."

"Did any of the other students seem upset or out of sorts?"

"Oh, no. Of course not. We all had a great time."

"Derek and Susanna are excellent hosts," Bradley said. "Their parties are always fun. They make their guests feel welcome."

"Yes, they do. Right at home. Did the kids who live next door crash the party the way they did the faculty get-together on Saturday?" I winked at Bradley and we shared a laugh.

The turn in the conversation seemed to relieve Gretchen. Her hunched shoulders relaxed, she grinned, and gave a soft snicker. "No, they didn't, but I've had encounters with them. Cute kids. Bit of an overbearing mother."

I turned to Bradley. "Has Vicki approached you about including her twins in a research project?"

"I haven't had the pleasure."

I laughed at his droll reply and, to my delight, Gretchen offered pertinent information unbidden.

"Vicki approached me. Called the department last week and asked for me. She said she and Derek had discussed including the girls in a study on twins and wondered, out of respect for Derek's legacy, if I'd be interested in conducting the research."

Good grief. Vicki is worse than the worst stage mother.

"I politely declined. I told Vicki my research plate is full—which is true—and that, going into my dissertation defense year, I wouldn't have any time for a new research project."

"Miranda's indulged her." Bradley nibbled on the last chunk of his bagel. "She sent Ashley to observe the family at the Hearth the other night."

"I hope it was just to appease Vicki and that it puts an end to her quest to see her daughters' names in an academic journal." Gretchen swiped a napkin across her lips.

That's not the only place Vicki wants to see Eliza's and Josie's names. She wants to see them on marquees, movie theater screens, and in the credits of every show on television.

"I agree." Gretchen and Bradley didn't need to know that I'd been present during Ashley's observation of the Shepards. They might suspect my questions were leading, like the next query I posed to Gretchen. "Will you also juggle teaching a class or two with the rest of your work next semester?"

Was that a slight twitch in her jaw? Did I strike a mandibular nerve?

"Yes. I'll teach a couple of classes."

"Courses that you've designed?" I gave Gretchen the best innocent look I could muster.

"No." Gretchen's tone dulled. "I'll be teaching an Intro to Psychology course and Intro to Developmental Psychology."

I attempted to cheer Gretchen, in case she hadn't poisoned Derek in an act of revenge. A sort of atonement for rubbing in the disappointment of not winning the Instructor Prize. "You might convince a few students not considering psychology to choose it for their major. Would you get a referral bonus if a student declares psychology their major after taking your class?"

Bradley and Gretchen chuckled.

"No. All I'd get is the satisfaction of introducing students to the fascinating inner workings of the human mind."

"Not a bad thing. You could inspire a future Sigmund Freud or Carl Jung."

"Better than being an influence for a future pop psychologist," Gretchen said.

"They're the worst." I enjoyed Bradley's and Gretchen's laughter. "Well, my friends, I better get these beverages back to my gals or I'll be in big trouble."

"What can they do?" Bradley asked with amusement. "You're the boss."

"The word *strike* is sometimes whispered when I don't make a timely coffee delivery."

"Not even the boss is immune from consequences," Gretchen said without a hint of her new adviser's spirit.

"Gretchen's still obviously disappointed about not winning the Instructor Prize," I said aloud to myself on the walk back to All Things.

The question is: Did Derek suffer the consequence of not giving Gretchen's application for the prize the department's top ranking?

Chapter Twenty-Seven

I have many photographs and keepsakes from my thirty-plus years on *Days and Nights*. I don't show off these items; my soap memorabilia was tucked away in albums and cabinets around the house. Knowing the treasures would impress Miranda, I pulled them from their "hiding" places and arranged them around my home. Photos with my co-stars went on the mantel. A vase that was a set piece in my character's living room was placed on my dining room table, complete with a bouquet of purple alstroemeria. The piece-de-resistance—my Daytime Emmy Award for Outstanding Lead Actress in a Drama Series—was moved from a shelf in the china cabinet to the living room table between the couch and a wing chair.

I polished my Emmy with the tail of my cotton shirt. I stood back, admired my decorations, and said a silent prayer that the artifacts of my life would loosen Miranda's tongue when it was time for me to ask the questions.

"May I?" Miranda asked thirty minutes later. She had zeroed in on the end table the moment she entered the living room. She stood with a slight lean forward, her hands inches from my gleaming, golden Emmy.

I dressed my response with a dash of noblesse oblige. "Of course."

"Ooh, it's heavy!" Miranda gazed at my award with awe. She struck the "I'd like to thank the Academy" pose so many do when they hold a trophy—or hairbrush, ladle, or can of air freshener.

Is she going to deliver a tear-filled acceptance speech?

Miranda's glance swept the room and landed on the mantel.

The Freudian Slip Murder

Clutching my award with both hands, she darted to the photo of one of my leading men and me. She pressed a finger against the frame's glass. "What a lovely photo of you and Alex Shelby. How many times were your characters married? To each other, I mean."

"Three." I snickered. "I don't know why I'm proud my character, Rachel, was married to the same man three times and entered marital union a total of six. But I am."

"You may be subconsciously ashamed you've never married and thus have inordinate pride that your soap character, with whom you are inextricably linked, married multiple times. It makes you feel good that men found her so attractive."

Mumbo jumbo. Blah blah. "Yeah. Maybe."

"It's healthy you don't think Rachel was a tramp or slut."

I wanted to yank my Emmy from Miranda's hands and bop her on the head with it. If there wasn't the danger of my Emmy getting damaged...

"Like you said, Rachel and I are inextricably linked. It would be a sort of self-loathing to call her a slut."

Miranda laughed with delight. "I adore your wit, Veronica." She moved to the couch and sat, my Emmy still in her hands. She leaned against the couch cushion and cradled the statuette as if it were an infant.

That's my baby! I steamed the whole way into the kitchen, through the pouring of two mugs of tea, the setting of slices of Entenmann's pound cake on a plate, and the return to the living room with the refreshments on a tray.

I set the tray on the coffee table and offered Miranda one of the mugs. She set the Emmy on the table; I oh-so-casually lifted it, along with the second mug, and sat in the wing chair. The Emmy I placed on the side table, within my reach and out of Miranda's easy grab. I didn't worry she'd break the statuette; I feared she'd tuck the award in her tote bag if I left the room again.

It was my turn to admire Miranda's work. "I'm impressed with your work on Asian American development. You've done some fascinating research on first-generation adolescents whose parents immigrated from—"

Miranda interrupted with a pleased look of surprise. "You've read my articles?"

"A couple, yes. Impressive."

"Thank you." Miranda dipped her head in gratitude and sipped her tea. "My father and his family emigrated from China when he was twelve. My research on Asian American development of children and adults is the focus of my career, but I enjoy variety in my work and projects that are the polar opposite of my usual research. For example, the article I'd like to write about how you and other actors develop your characters."

Another paper featuring me. I hope I don't become overexposed in the psychology journals. "Wow. What other actors have you booked for interviews?" I knew the answer, but sipped my tea, blew the dust off my not-used-in-decades ingénue glance, and bestowed it on Miranda.

"You're my lucky first!" Miranda said, unabashed. "And I was hoping you'd put in a good word for me with your former castmates. Alex Shelby, Melanie Hughes..."

"I don't know how available they are for interviews," I said, "but I'll mention it the next time I talk with them." Alex, I knew, would agree in a heartbeat.

"I'd be in your debt forever."

Let's start the payback now. I took another sip of tea and shifted the conversation. "Mark told me that one of your PhD candidates has been awarded a coveted Instructor Prize."

"Is Mark jealous?" Miranda winked. "We're all immensely proud of Ray. He will make a big mark in the field."

"Did any other PhD candidates from the psychology department apply for the prize?"

"Oh, yes. All four who are going into their dissertation year applied." Miranda reeled off the applicants' names, including Gretchen's.

Dotsie's theory! "Any hurt feelings among the three who didn't get the prize?"

"None expressed. Though, I'm sure..." Miranda's expression turned coy. "Do you ask because of personal experience, Veronica? There were many years when you were overlooked for an Emmy nomination or didn't win the statuette when you were nominated. How did that make you feel?" She gestured to my glimmering gold award. "There must have been jealousy when you won this beauty. You must have wanted another."

"There was disappointment but never jealousy on my part. My friends deserved their nominations and awards." *Enough about me.* "Mark explained that if a department has more than one applicant for the prize, the chairperson will rank the applicants. Did Derek ask his colleagues for their opinions—"

"No, he didn't. Oh, I see what you're doing." Miranda shot me an astute glance. "Have you added three names to your suspect list? Doctoral students angry because Derek didn't rank them first for the prize?"

"Why not? I may not have a degree in psychology, but I've learned a lot about human nature over my five decades of life. What seems like a baseless motive to a rational person could be the reason a person not thinking rationally took another's life."

Ha! You may have conducted hours of research, but I've been out there in the real world. Portraying the beautiful, ugly human condition every day!

"You're right, Veronica. You've had more contact with the criminal mind than I have." Miranda's tone turned grave. "I hate to think that a student poisoned Derek. That one of them would've thrown away a promising career all because they didn't get a prize. I try not to dwell on the possibility that someone from our team killed Derek. It's too awful to consider."

I regarded the melancholy in Miranda's downcast glance and realized her cheerfulness and competence over the last few days was a mask concealing her worry and sorrow. She had become the leader of the psychology department, but she was burdened by the weight of Derek's death and its implications for her colleagues and students.

I knew just how to lift her spirits. "Would you like me to take a photo of you holding my Emmy?"

My gesture worked like a charm. Miranda's gloom lifted and she wasted no time reaching for the statuette.

Chapter Twenty-Eight

I returned to All Things after Miranda's visit and spent the afternoon hours assisting customers and discussing summer window displays, promotions, and product orders with Claire and the staff. At four p.m. I received a phone call from one of my canasta buddies.

"Veronica! I have information that you will find very informative to the professor's murder case!"

The excited pitch of Dotsie's voice caused my heart to beat faster. "What is it?"

"I can't tell you over the phone. Come to my house tonight. Seven-thirty."

"All right." I grew wary, leery that time spent at Dotsie's would be time wasted. However, that she may've hit the target with her suspicion of Gretchen.

Bemused, I slipped my cell into my pocket. I entertained the image of Dotsie, dressed in a trench coat and wearing a man's fedora, standing at a pay phone on a dark, deserted street, fog swirling around her. She relayed her message to me with one hand cupped between her mouth and the phone's mouthpiece.

The top-secret spy scenario, played out in black and white, entertained me. With Dotsie's impassioned delivery of her request, I imagined she envisioned herself in a similar fashion.

"This should be good," I muttered.

The last time I'd visited Dotsie's home—she'd hosted the canasta game four weeks earlier—the house and yard had been decorated for Easter. Plastic eggs tied to ribbons dangled from the three maple trees in her front yard and inside the house, each room had a display of baskets filled with pink, green, yellow, or purple plastic grass, chocolate eggs, jelly beans, and marshmallow chicks. She had also put out her collection of stuffed bunny toys. She'd received a stuffed toy every Easter of her seventy-plus years.

"At least one," Sandy whispered as she attempted to count all the bunnies.

"Now we know stuffed rabbits reproduce *as* fast as live bunnies do," I'd muttered.

The Easter decorations were gone and Dotsie had trimmed her home in patriotic colors in preparation for the Memorial Day and July Fourth holidays. In addition to the U.S. flag that always hung from a bracket attached to a post near the front door, metal red, white, and blue stars had replaced the plastic eggs dangling from the tree branches.

I checked out the selection of shiny red-white-and-blue striped lawn decorations on my walk to the door. There were at least fifty pinwheels poked into the grass, all motionless because of the still evening air.

Dotsie answered the ring of the doorbell not in a trench coat and fedora but in dark blue jeans and a navy-blue T-shirt with *U.S.A.* printed across the chest in red.

The theme continues.

"You have your own mini-wind farm." I stepped into the house. *Do her neighbors embrace Dotsie's whimsy or are they members of the not in my backyard—or front lawn—crowd?*

"Ha!" Dotsie shut the door. "You should see them when they're all spinning."

Thank goodness she doesn't have a collection of patriotic wind chimes.

"Maybe I will when you host the game next week. So what do you have on the murder case?"

Dotsie gave a knowing nod. "There's someone you need to talk with. Follow me."

She led me down the hall to her family room. I shouldn't have been surprised by the life-sized cardboard cutout of America's Uncle Sam that stood in front of the sliding door, but I was startled by the figure's pointing finger and glaring expression.

"This is Rena." Dotsie gestured to a young woman standing by the couch.

Rena came forward and offered her hand. Her brown-eyed gaze met mine over her soft handshake.

"Rena is my neighbor's daughter. She works the night desk at the Farley Inn. She's been there a couple of months."

The inn, located not too far down Orchard Street from All Things, was Barton's elegantly-appointed establishment for overnight guests to our village.

"Terrific. Congratulations." I gave a polite smile to Rena, who looked to be in her mid- twenties.

"Sit down." Dotsie made a gesture with her arms. "I'll get you a ginger ale, Veronica."

"Thanks."

Rena sat on the couch and took a sip from a glass of cola. She gave me an amused look. "Mrs. Beattie obviously didn't tell you anything."

"Dotsie is a woman of mystery." I lowered myself to the edge of the brown recliner, leaned forward, and spoke in a low voice. "She said that you have information important to the Derek Morley case. Is that true or an exaggeration? Did she blackmail or bribe you to come here or are you a kind soul humoring her?"

Rena giggled. "There were no payments. And I *may* have information."

Dotsie returned and placed a tall glass filled with ginger ale on the coffee table. She scooted around the corner of the table and sat on the couch. "Rena saw Susanna Rafferty at the Farley. Dining with a gentleman who was *not* her husband."

Dotsie does have useful information! Forgive me, Father, for being a Doubting Veronica.

I reigned in my excitement. Susanna's dinner could've been an innocent meeting and be irrelevant to the case. "Do you know the man's name?"

"Eric Nelson. He stayed at the inn one night that week."

Eric Nelson. The renowned historian who was Susanna's friend and college classmate.

"The author," Dotsie added. "He writes terrific biographies."

"I know. I met him at Derek's memorial service. He and Susanna attended college together."

"Ahh! Former sweethearts." Dotsie's tone was suggestive, her expression very cat that ate the canary.

"I don't know if they ever dated."

"Mr. Nelson stayed at the inn the night of the memorial service too."

"Did Susanna visit him that night too? A midnight rendezvous?" Dotsie asked. "Comfort for the grieving widow?"

"Dotsie!" I gave her a chastising look and returned to Rena. "What night was it when you saw Susanna and Eric Nelson having dinner together?"

"Wednesday." Rena gave the date.

"Are you sure it was Susanna Rafferty?"

"Yes." Rena's emphatic nod put a swing in her light-brown ponytail. "She asked me to call Mr. Nelson and tell him she'd arrived for dinner. When Mr. Nelson came down to the lobby, they threw their arms around each other and hugged for a good thirty seconds."

"A cozy college reunion for two," Dotsie said.

I ignored her innuendo. "Go on, Rena."

"First, they sat on the couch in the lobby and had a drink. Then they went in for dinner."

"A two-and-a-half-hour dinner," Dotsie added.

I asked, "What did they do after dinner?"

"They went up to Mr. Nelson's room." Rena lowered her gaze to the table.

"Susanna was up there with him for more than an hour," Dotsie said.

Her power of suggestion was beginning to work its effect on me. What would the pair be doing in Eric's room? They could have had an after-dinner beverage on the comfortable couch in the lobby and continued their conversation from dinner.

"Did they ask for a liqueur or coffee to be sent up to the room? Brandy or Irish coffee?" I asked.

"Maybe just whipped cream."

"Dotsie!"

"No, they didn't order room service." Rena clasped her hands together. "Look, I don't usually gossip about the inn's guests. I saw Susanna's name in the newspaper article about her husband's poisoning and thought, you know..."

"I know."

"You're not going to tell my boss that I broke the confidentiality of a guest, are you? I'd be fired!"

"I won't say a word," I said.

"You're a source," Dotsie said. "Veronica protects her sources. And my lips are sealed."

"Let's just hope Uncle Sam doesn't squeal." With my thumb I gestured to the patriotic cutout looming over my shoulder.

I stood with Dotsie on her front porch and watched Rena trot across the street to her parents' house. Bracing myself with a deep breath, I said, "Dotsie, you may have been on to something about Gretchen."

"Girl Power Punch!" Dotsie emphasized her declaration by punching the air with her fist. "So what'd you learn on the tattle-tale?"

"She *didn't* win a big prize." I related the awards information and Gretchen's demeanor at the bakery.

"*Quid pro quo* doesn't always go according to plan." Dotsie clicked her tongue. "Gretchen gave but didn't receive. She learned a tough lesson and now she won't be giving them at Arden. Maybe nowhere else, if she punched—"

I took a few steps back to avoid Dotsie's right-hook swipe at the air and had a jab of pity for Gretchen. "Remember, this is all a theory. Gretchen may be nothing more than a snitch."

"That's right. Rena's information points to another suspect. Does Derek's history-loving spouse love history a little too much?"

"Keep that under your hat," I warned Dotsie. "Keep all of this under your hat. Gretchen may have done nothing more than sulk about not winning the Instructor Prize. And Susanna and Eric's retreat to his room—"

"*Bed*room—"

"May've been perfectly innocent."

"They sat on separate ends of the bed and talked about George and Martha Washington's se—"

"Dotsie." My voice was stern, like a referee's warning to boxers to go to their respective corners.

Dotsie beamed with delight. "You know, George and Martha didn't have children of their own. So maybe they didn't have such a hot—"

"Dotsie!"

"I hear you, Veronica. I'll keep all this under my hat. I have a ten-gallon hat that'll do."

"Perfect," I said with large serving of irony.

I gave Dotsie a good night kiss on the cheek. An image of Dotsie trotting along Orchard Street wearing a ten-gallon hat and a cat-that-ate-the-canary expression got stuck in my mind. She was fully-clothed, too, of course.

Wouldn't want that image in my brain before I go to bed.

What if Dotsie was right about either Gretchen or Susanna? The possibility that one of her theories identified Derek's murderer amused me.

Why not? If I can solve murders, anyone can. If Dotsie solves this case, she can take over the role of Barton's amateur sleuth.

I tooted the car horn in farewell to Dotsie, who waved to me from the porch, and backed out of the driveway. The image of Dotsie strutting down Orchard, now with one of those pinwheels stuck in the band of her ten-gallon hat, fixed itself in my head. I stuck a flag in her hand and soundtracked the scene with "Yankee Doodle Dandy."

If Dotsie was right, I'd recommend that she be the grand marshal in the July Fourth parade.

Chapter Twenty-Nine

Without one detail, I would've considered Susanna and Eric's dinner nothing more than a meal and conversation between longtime friends. It was the hour-long visit to Eric's room that prevented me from ending the scene.

In my imagination, I pictured a *Do Not Disturb* sign hanging on the outside of his door. In the room's interior, a champagne bottle chilling in a bucket of ice. Red rose petals strewn across the bed. White votive candles filling the room with soft light.

"Stop!"

I was already stopped at a traffic light on Orchard Street. I rested my forehead against my palm. *Did I waste an hour at Dotsie's? Do I want that hour of my life back or did Rena just supply a motive for Susanna to kill her husband?*

The light changed to green, and I continued down Orchard.

Why was Eric at the inn? Was he traveling through the area and stopped overnight? Why didn't he stay with Susanna and Derek if he and Susanna were such good friends?

When Susanna introduced me to Eric at the memorial service, there was no remark about how they had seen each other only a week before when Susanna mentioned that they saw each other several times a year.

I arrived home and pulled into my detached garage. I hurried into the house and went straight to the television room, where I'd left my laptop.

I typed *Eric Nelson* into the browser's search box and was delighted when dozens of links appeared on the screen. I clicked on the link to Eric's *Wikipedia* page and went straight to the *Personal Life* section of his biography. It was a short paragraph. He was born and raised in Pennsylvania, was a devout fan of the Pittsburgh Steelers and Pirates, and had earned his Eagle Scout badge by leading a beautification project for his local historical society. There was no mention of a wife—past or present. His current home was in Annapolis, Maryland.

I returned to the results page and clicked on the *News* tab. "Maybe there will be a recent article giving a reason for his visit to the area." I thought Eric may have given a commencement address at a college in upstate New York, Vermont, or western Massachusetts. Or perhaps he was on a research trip. *Work on a book on the Adams family—John, John Quincy, and Abigail?*

The most recent news item on Eric was from March, when he participated in a panel discussion on Theodore Roosevelt's presidency at Syracuse University. Susanna was also on the panel.

"Hmmm."

I looked at a few other sites that mentioned Eric and finished on a few-years-old interview he did with *The Saturday Evening Post*. A photograph attached to the piece piqued my interest. In the photo the historian stood on a porch, his back leaning against the waist-high white railing. The pose showed off a majestic background of a lake and trees heavy with autumnal foliage.

The caption read: *Nelson at his retreat on New Hampshire's Lake Winnipesaukee.*

"So Eric is *that* friend who offered Susanna the use of his New England getaway."

Would he also be in residence during Susanna's visit?

"What's Dotsie's grand theory this time?" Mark asked. He'd answered my phone call on the second ring.

"This time she has facts to back it up. *Maybe.*"

"Let's hear it."

"Dotsie has a witness to a cozy dinner between Susanna and Eric Nelson at the Farley the week before Derek died." I recounted everything Rena had told me.

Mark was quiet for a minute after I finished. "It could all be circumstantial evidence. There could be a reasonable explanation for the visit to Eric's room."

I wished I could see Mark's face. He sounded troubled by this latest suggestion of Susanna's possible involvement in Derek's death. "I know. I agree. Did Susanna mention that Eric would be in Barton that week? Did she say she would be meeting him for dinner?"

"No." Mark's tone held no accusation, but that Susanna hadn't made casual mention of seeing her friend could be a damaging fact against her. "Dotsie will keep this to herself?"

"Yes. We both promised Rena we would be careful with the information. She's concerned it will get back to her boss that she gossiped about a guest."

"Gossip. I've never heard so much in my life."

"Lucky you," I said. "It was all around me at *Days and Nights*. Showbiz gossip is the worst. I tried my best to stay above it. I'm proud I never spread it, but I'm a little disappointed I was never the subject of some of the juicier tidbits. I was the good girl of the cast."

Mark laughed. "I'm glad I've never had to deal with such a fruitful grapevine."

"What do you gossip about around the watercooler?"

"George Washington and Mary Philipse. Thomas Jefferson and Sally Hemings. King Edward and Wallis Simpson."

"You shameless gossipmongers."

Chapter Thirty

The ring of my cell and Susanna's name on the screen prompted a flashback to my elementary school days at Saint Augustine Catholic school.

It's recess and I'm on the playground with Carol and two of our friends. We're playing hopscotch. I toss my pebble and hop across the boxes. Someone yells that my foot touched one of the chalk-drawn lines. I claim I didn't.

I can still hear the clamor of the bell. I turn. Sister Helen, the principal, stands a few feet away, with her ever-present stern expression and the gold hand bell she rings whenever she wants students' attention. Or to scare the heck out of us.

I've been caught cheating! I fear I'll be sentenced to no recess for a week. Or cleaning every chalkboard in the school for a month. Or the worst, a punishment I've never witnessed that has become the stuff of schoolyard legend: ten whacks on the back of my hand with a wooden yardstick.

Susanna knows I know about her cozy dinner with Eric.

I answer the call with trepidation, my heart palpitating and my stomach twisting into a knot.

How could she know I know? Calm down.

"Good morning, Veronica!"

I wished Susanna the same and asked how she was.

"I awoke this morning with a craving to sink my teeth into a Hearth cheeseburger. Will you join me for lunch? My treat."

"I never say no to a cheeseburger."

We arranged to meet at the Hearth at twelve-thirty and I ended the call with a sigh of relief. Of course Susanna had no idea of the report I'd received from Rena. And Sister Helen didn't ring the bell to call everyone's attention to my sinful behavior. It was the end of recess and she had summoned her charges to lineup by grade for our march back to class.

With a hunger for answers and ground beef grilled and topped with cheddar cheese, I crossed Orchard Street and walked the few yards to the Hearth. Susanna was already there, seated at a table by the window.

"The police haven't reported any progress. I'm nervous the case has gone cold," she said after our server had taken our soft drink and burger orders.

"Don't be. The police keep a tight lid on their investigations. They don't tell everything. Not even to the family." *Or the resident amateur sleuth.*

"But what if they truly haven't any leads? I lie awake at nights wondering how they will ever be able to prove a case against someone. Derek *ingested* the murder weapon. There are no fingerprints because there are so many incidental prints in my house and the psychology department. Everyone has antifreeze in their garages. Finding a bottle won't implicate anyone." Susanna flourished her hands in a helpless gesture. "Someone will have to confess and who's going to do that? The killer must be very satisfied. Justice might never be served."

"It will. A lot goes on behind the scenes that the public never sees. We think it's quiet, and then one morning the newspaper headline announces that the killer's been caught. Facts come together very quickly."

We put the conversation on pause while our server set our sodas on the table.

"You would know better than I. Have you uncovered anything since last we spoke?" Susanna asked.

"Nothing." I took a deep sip of my ginger ale and wondered how I'd get the conversation around to Eric.

"How's business today?"

"Typical for a weekday with no holiday in sight."

"What a change for you after so many years acting."

"A big change. I had no idea what I'd do after the soap was canceled. I had no offers of new work because of my age. I thought I'd end up working in my mother's bookstore, stacking shelves and handling the register."

Susanna gave a sympathetic nod. "And you ended up with your own shelves to stock and with a cash register to call your own."

"And a staff with the patience to teach me everything I needed to know about running a retail business."

"Well, thank goodness for tenure. Arden isn't going anywhere, and I can't be fired. I can even take a semester or year's sabbatical and won't lose my job."

"Are you thinking of taking a sabbatical? You haven't mentioned your plans beyond the summer."

"I don't know. It won't be next semester since I'm committed to teaching my scheduled fall classes." Susanna paused and gave a seconds-long contemplative glance at her glass before she raised it to her lips and took a drink of her soda. "Several friends have given me the standard advice of not making any big decisions until a year has passed. I know that applies to selling the house or quitting my job. I don't plan on doing either anytime soon. I want to teach for a long while and I want to stay in the house for the rest of my life. I hope I'm able to fulfill both goals."

We enjoyed our drinks for a moment and Susanna continued.

"Some friends have told me to focus on my work and others have told me it wouldn't be good to drown myself in it to get through the grieving process. I have to find meaning in something other than work."

"Did someone from the psychology department impart that advice?"

"Miranda!"

"Be careful. You might end up the star subject in a research project."

Susanna laughed. "The thing is, I have plenty of work to dive into. I have the book on Abigail Adams I've been planning for a while. And I've been asked to collaborate on a book about presidential marriages."

"That sounds interesting."

"It would be a high-profile project. My partner would be my friend, Eric."

I got a charge of excitement at the mention of Eric. "Fantastic!"

Sometimes I have to ask the questions. Sometimes I just have to listen.

"The book would be the source material for a documentary," Susanna said. "Eric, you probably know, has had three of his biographies made into documentaries."

"I've watched them on PBS."

"This would be a major project for me. It would consume a great deal of my free time."

"Would it be a burden?" I asked.

"No. I would lose myself in the work, in the best way. I couldn't contain my excitement when Eric proposed the project."

I, too, struggled to control my glee over this marvelous turn in the conversation. "How long ago did he make this proposal?"

"Two and a half weeks ago. The Wednesday before Derek died." Susanna paused, her expression turning reflective. "Eric came to Barton to discuss the project with me. He stayed at the Farley. I met him there for dinner."

Our server set our plates of cheeseburgers and fries on the table. For a few minutes we occupied ourselves with squeezing ketchup over our food and taking our first tastes of our juicy burgers.

"Did Derek join you?" I felt a dab of ketchup on the corner of my mouth and cleared it with a dainty swipe of my napkin.

"No. Eric told me he wanted to talk *shop* with me. It wasn't an explicit request to exclude Derek, but I understood his meaning. Derek wouldn't have gone, anyway. He and Eric got along fine, but as Eric gained acclaim for his work, Derek grew jealous of him. No surprise." Susanna paused to sip her drink.

During the pause I thanked my lucky stars that Mark never envied my acting awards and the attention I occasionally received from Barton residents and visitors. Though he'd tease that I still lived in the land of soaps when my imagination ran wild, but he'd say it with love and an affectionate twinkle in his eyes.

"Derek was never rude to Eric. He just...well...always grew tired when the conversation was about Eric's work. Derek was happy to stay at home while I went to the Farley. He claimed he had end-of-term work to do." She bit into her burger and savored its flavors. I did the same with my burger.

"Eric and I talked about the project for more than two hours. We had one idea after another. I envisioned not only writing the words but also hearing the narrator read them in the documentary. After dinner, we went up to his room. He showed me the advance copy of his upcoming book on the Reconstruction years. I've read several drafts, but it's always exciting to see a hard copy of the book with its cover."

Aha. That's why the pair retreated to Eric's room. I felt like a fool. My soap operatic vision of candles, rose petals and champagne—plus Dotsie's whipped cream—dissolved into two strait-laced historians thumbing through a galley of text on events that happened more than a century ago. The whispered sweet-nothings became normal-volume voices debating the validity of Andrew Johnson's impeachment.

"What did Derek think of the project?"

"You know the answer, Veronica."

"He didn't want you to do it."

Susanna nodded. "He thought it would take up too much of my time. Eric and I would work on it over this summer. Derek and I didn't have any set plans for the break other than our individual research and writing projects. We'd probably go to Cape Cod for a week or two like we always did, but that was it. Suddenly, after I told him about the collaboration, he had a list of activities we'd do together. Day trips. A trip up to Canada. He wanted to jam pack the summer so I'd hardly have a minute to breathe."

Her eyes grew misty. "It's difficult to acknowledge that my husband was jealous of my career. It's particularly hard to admit Derek's flaws now."

"I'm sorry." I reached across the table and patted her hand.

Susanna gave a weak smile and swiped away her tears before they slipped down her cheeks.

"Were you going to write the book with Eric, regardless of Derek's objection?"

"I hadn't given Eric my answer before Derek died. I was in *negotiations* with Derek about it. I offered schedules for when I'd work with Eric and when I'd spend time with him. I promised I wouldn't be away from home for more than ten days at a time. Derek turned it into a choice between the book or him. My career or him. He elevated it to an existential crisis for our marriage." A woeful expression clouded Susanna's face.

"Would Derek have come around and realized what a wonderful opportunity this project was for you? Wouldn't he have eventually supported you and been proud of you? Wouldn't he have put himself in your place and understood you would have been behind him one-hundred percent?"

"He may have. But I couldn't afford to give him that time. Eric wanted my answer within the week."

Susanna took a nibble from her burger. I felt terrible; she had looked forward to enjoying it and now the meal was spoiled.

"The day after our barbecue, I made my decision. That evening, I told Derek I was going to write the book. He yelled that I was choosing my career over our marriage. He had gotten home first and had already had a couple of drinks. He was tipsy, or so I thought. I took a walk to cool off and give him time to do the same. I still believed his objection was all bluster and ego and he'd come around. Except he didn't."

Susanna's expression grew melancholic, and she shifted her gaze out the window.

She continued after a minute. "After the memorial service I told Eric I'd write the book. And ever since I've felt I'm betraying Derek's final wishes."

Man, Derek did a number on Susanna's self-esteem.

"If you feel the need to atone, dedicate the book to his memory."

Susanna grinned. "Perhaps your second career should've been therapist rather than shopkeeper."

It's a good thing I'm not a therapist. If I were, I'd have to keep everything she just said confidential.

I made an exaggerated shrug. "Maybe a third career."

Susanna laughed and took a generous bite of her burger. We finished the meal over conversation on lighter topics.

I returned to All Things with more than the food in my stomach to digest.

Chapter Thirty-One

I called Noelle soon after returning to All Things. "Are you available for a chat?"

"You can buy me an apple martini at Flannery's at four-thirty."

She sounded neither tired nor exasperated, but I asked, "Has it been a day?"

"No. I just want to brag that I had a drink with a famous actress."

My fame continues to precede me. I hope Noelle will be this honest in her answers to my harder questions.

"An apple martini at four-thirty it is."

Two blocks from campus, Flannery's steakhouse was popular with Arden's faculty and administrators. Mark and I had dined there several times, but we'd never enjoyed drinks at the bar.

Arriving before the five o'clock happy hour, Noelle and I had our pick of seats and chose a table by the window. I joined her in ordering an apple martini

"Cheers." Noelle tipped her glass against mine.

I murmured a salutation and for a half-minute we enjoyed our cocktails in companionable silence.

Noelle munched on a pretzel from the bowl the bartender had set on the table. "I hear you were a hit with Miranda, Bradley, and Ashley. They all raved about how honest and wonderful you were during their interviews."

"I enjoyed my time with all of them. Arden must be proud of its impressive faculty and students."

"We are." Noelle sipped her cocktail.

"How long have you been at Arden?" I asked.

"Thirty years. I've been the psychology department's admin for the last fifteen."

"So you know everyone on the faculty well. And I suppose you get a lot of intellectual stimulation from working in the department that studies the human mind."

"No two minds think alike," Noelle said with a laugh. "And I have a front-row seat to observing the observers."

Great segue for the reason we'd bellied up to this bar. "Last week you told me that no one in the psychology department had a reason to poison Derek."

"I did." I noted that she didn't underscore her earlier statement with a fresh defense of her colleagues.

"I've since learned about his contentious relationship with Ashley—"

"That was settled weeks ago."

"I know. But was there any lingering resentment between the two? Any passive-aggressive remarks either aimed at the other?"

"Ashley behaved admirably. She concentrated on her work and was respectful to Derek in the interactions I witnessed."

"And Derek?"

Noelle sighed. "He made a few remarks—yes, passive-aggressive—about Ashley's complaints against him. He never mentioned her by name. He made a fuss over Ray, who just won the Instructor Prize—"

'Mark told me about the awards. Congratulations to Ray and the department."

"We're proud of Ray. Derek bragged about how *all* of his students succeed under his guidance. How more of his graduate and PhD advisees have won awards than any other adviser in the department."

"But who's keeping score?"

Noelle snickered at my sarcasm. "Derek had a competitive streak a mile wide."

"Gretchen also won a stipend. Good for her."

"Yes." Noelle sighed and swirled her cocktail around in its glass. "She was disappointed, though. She had high hopes for the Instructor Prize."

"Oh?"

Noelle sipped her drink. "I think she assumed she'd be the department's big winner."

"Because of Derek's record of awards success?"

"In part, yes. But Gretchen has a healthy ego and an abundance of self-confidence."

"Did she make any remarks after the awards' announcements? Passive-aggressive or otherwise?" I asked.

"Not that I heard. She gave Ray what appeared to be sincere congratulations on his award."

Yeah, like the sincere *applause we nominees give to the winner. Well, some of us were* sincere...

"No anger at Derek? Gretchen may have thought he gave Ray a heartier recommendation than the endorsement he gave her. True or not."

"Derek always placed more importance on the quality of the candidate's proposed course, not on the candidate."

"Mark read me the full description of Ray's class, but I confess the subject of behavioral analysis is a bit over my head."

Noelle laughed. "It's a mouthful. Read it over a couple times on your own and you'll understand it, I'm sure."

"You're kind. What was the theme of Gretchen's proposed course?"

"Adolescent Development in the Age of Social Media. A worthy topic, but one Bradley covers in one of his courses."

"Is that where Gretchen got her idea?" I asked.

Noelle grew circumspect. "Oh, I have no idea."

She doesn't want to accuse Gretchen of stealing Bradley's idea. But did Derek? "Would Bradley have discussed the proposed classes with Derek? You know, remind Derek that social media was his area of expertise?"

"His turf?" Noelle smirked. "The faculty discussed all the proposed courses and which would complement the department course schedule. And every year a professor will point out the similarity between a proposed course and their own. They'd generously call it cryptomnesia. Unconscious plagiarism, for us laypeople."

"Cryptomnesia. You learn something new every day."

Noelle and I had a giggle over the term and she clinked her glass against mine.

"Are the *plagiarized* professors more flattered than furious that a student committed cryptomnesia and copied them?" I asked.

"The faculty always has a good laugh over the similarities." Noelle gave me a side-eye. "If you're thinking that Gretchen or another student upset over not winning an award poisoned Derek—"

"I am," I said, unabashed by her scolding glance. "*Someone* had a motive."

Noelle shrugged off my push back. "Yes. But I don't think the rejection of a course or the loss of a prize is sufficient motive." She gave me a pointed look. "You actors know about rejection. You go through lots of auditions for roles you don't get. And only one person wins the Emmy. One winner, several losers. Has a casting director or producer or Emmy voter ever been murdered?"

"No, but actors have creative minds. There've been plenty of murderous thoughts. I'm sure many of them elaborate and planned to the minutest detail. Coping mechanism." I savored my drink and Noelle's laughter. "Gretchen told me that she wants to spend her career at Arden. Do you foresee her joining the department after she earns her PhD?" I asked.

Noelle finished her cocktail. "I do. Gretchen's a homegrown talent. She'd be a terrific addition to the faculty."

I took the final sip of my drink and mulled Noelle's closing remark.

What if Derek had a conversation with Gretchen about her intellectual dishonesty? Tell her she wasn't Arden material and would never be a faculty member?

How funny that it was Vicki who told me about the driveway scene between Derek and Gretchen. Derek scorned Vicki's quote unquote research. Did he also disparage Gretchen's? Or...

Did Derek not endorse Gretchen's application because her class was similar to a course taught by Bradley, not Derek? Was Derek jealous because Gretchen "imitated" the younger, handsomer, media-acclaimed Bradley?

I reflected back to Bradley and Gretchen's meeting at Rizzuto's. Did a romantic flame flicker between the professor and PhD candidate? Did Derek's treatment of Gretchen—and other women in the department—prompt Bradley to action?

I tossed in a final question. Did Derek not only quash Gretchen's chance at winning the Instructor Prize but also her ambition to join Arden's faculty?

Did, did, did. So many in the case. One of them pointed to the poisoner. But which one?

Chapter Thirty-Two

"So? What's the update on the professor and her dinner companion?" Dotsie stretched her long legs and waggled her eyebrows.

Sandy, Myrtle, Ella, and Madeline gave me eager looks. It was the night of our weekly canasta game, and it was my turn to host the gathering.

"Susanna had an affair?" Sandy asked, wide-eyed with surprise.

"Oh, I hate to hear that." Madeline shook her head and clicked her tongue.

"No!" I startled everyone, including myself, with the loud exclamation. "No." I turned to face Dotsie, who sat on the opposite end of my living room couch. "That dinner was a meal between friends, with a bit of business talk."

"What about the post-meal visit to Eric Nelson's room?" Dotsie asked. "More *business* talk?"

"Eric Nelson? The historian?" The esteemed historian's involvement in the story raised Ella's interest.

"Yes. He and Susanna attended college together." I paused. "This is between us, okay? Not to be repeated. Eric came to Barton the Wednesday before Derek died to discuss a project with Susanna. He stayed at the Farley. Eric invited Susanna to dinner at the inn and asked her to collaborate with him on a book about presidential marriages. The book will be the source material for a documentary."

"How wonderful!" Madeline clapped twice. The dismay she displayed over Susanna's assumed adultery had faded into excitement over a sanctioned union of two minds.

"I look forward to reading this book," Ella said.

Madeline added, "And watching the documentary."

Dotsie, despite the fizzle of her theory, tried to support the hypothesis's back end. "So they talked about the book for two-and-a-half hours over dinner. You want us to believe they continued that talk for another hour in the bedroom?"

"No. They discussed the post-Civil War years in the bedroom. They went to Eric's room so he could show Susanna the advanced copy of his latest book." I fell into a fit of giggles. "It's on the Reconstruction era."

"Eggheads." Sandy, who sat between Dotsie and me, set her drink on the coffee table. Her jerking shoulders telegraphed her own peals of laughter. She fell back against the couch and we leaned against each other in full submission to our silly humor.

Madeline, Ella, and Myrtle joined our laughter and, within seconds, so did Dotsie. After a minute, we were all wiping our eyes and reaching for our cocktails.

"It could all be an elaborate ruse." Dotsie enjoyed a sip of her drink. "Those *eggheads* are smart. If they can string thousands of words together into a tome on Reconstruction or Martha Washington or whatever historical period they want, they can also compose a convincing cover story for their illicit trysts."

"Here we go with the conspiracy theory." I groaned and checked the time on my phone. The lasagna in my oven would be ready soon.

Myrtle defended her canasta partner. "Dotsie may be correct."

"Or they could really have discussed the book project, which made Derek jealous," I said.

"Really?" Madeline clicked her tongue. "Terrible."

"Yep. Susanna told me yesterday over lunch at the Hearth. He didn't want her to work with Eric."

Dotsie jabbed her index finger in the air. "And she poisoned him!" Her pronouncement held a note of triumph.

"To be determined. Another suspect has joined the lineup.

Gretchen Smith, another of the PhD candidates Derek advised." I told the ladies about Gretchen's application for the Instructor Prize, her loss, and Vicki's observations of Gretchen and Derek's interaction the night of the student party.

"Derek killed her shot at the prize, so Gretchen *killed* him!" Dotsie proclaimed.

"Wow," Sandy said, "Derek had a big problem with women."

"It seems so." I stood and picked up my empty glass. "Dinner will be served in five minutes."

We reconvened around the dining room table with plates of lasagna and slices of warmed Italian bread. We ate and discussed the murder case for a few minutes more until we turned to more pleasant dinner conversation.

After dinner Sandy and I cleared the dishes from the table and carried them to the kitchen. I transferred the lasagna left in the serving dish to three containers, wrapped the remaining slices of bread in foil, and popped the packages into the freezer. Sandy scraped and rinsed the dinner plates and stacked them in the dishwasher. She wiped down the countertops and swept stray food bits from the dining table with my crumb pan and brush.

We went back to the dining room, where the ladies had rearranged the chairs for the canasta game. Three decks of playing cards were stacked in the center of the table. Sandy took a seat and I was lowering myself into the chair across from her when the doorbell rang.

"Someone smelled the delicious lasagna and has come for a plate," Madeline said.

"Don't touch those cards," I said, tossing my canasta gang a faux-severe glance.

The bell was pressed twice more before I was out of the dining room.

"Maybe it's the police come to break up our raucous party."

Myrtle offered the dash of irony.

"Or to arrest Veronica," Dotsie said, chortling. "It was the soap diva who poisoned the professor!"

The bell blasted a fourth time.

Through the sidelights beside my front door I caught a glimpse of a figure on the porch, but the gauzy curtain covering the window panes prevented me from seeing who it was. I opened the door and came face-to-face with Ashley, whose cheeks were red and tearstained.

"What did you tell the police?" Her voice was a half-wail, half-screech.

"What?"

"What did you tell the police? They're interrogating Miranda at the police station!"

"Is everything okay?" Sandy stood near the stairs, steps from the door.

"No, it's not!" Ashley cried.

"Come in." I waved Ashley into the hall and with a gentle touch guided her into the living room. Sandy followed; the rest of the canasta club were already in the room.

I made the introductions while Sandy hustled into the dining room and returned with a chair. She steered Dotsie into it and took the spot on the couch beside Ashley. I sat on Ashley's left.

I handed the PhD candidate a cocktail napkin from the stack on the coffee table. "What about Miranda and the police?"

"I told you. They're interrogating her. Her lawyer's there! She'll probably be arrested!"

I stroked her back. "Relax. Take a breath." I paused and allowed Ashley a moment to calm. "Start at the beginning. What happened?"

Ashley blotted her cheeks and gave the group a circumspect look. "I was supposed to have dinner at her house. We were going to discuss my dissertation and summer classes."

"Hmmm." Dotsie's noise leaned toward the accusative.

I shot her a scolding look.

"Veronica told us a bit about your research project." Madeline's kind voice smoothed away Dotsie's suspicious manner. "How fascinating. I admire you so much, Ashley. When my sister and I were your age," she gestured at Ella, "women weren't encouraged to pursue Master's and PhD degrees."

"Women weren't even encouraged to attend college, unless it was to earn a teaching or nursing degree," Myrtle said.

Ashley's distress morphed into anger. "The patriarchy's still in place. Women can pursue advanced degrees, but the men are still in charge."

"As evidenced by Professor Morley's disregard for your work and demand that you give him credit for it." Dotsie sat up straighter and leveled her gaze on Ashley.

"I didn't poison him!" Ashley said, the pitch of her voice high enough to alert the neighborhood dogs.

"No one is accusing you." Sandy laid her hand on Ashley's shoulder. "You were to have dinner with Miranda..."

"Yes, but when I got there, she was on her way out. She said she the police had just called and asked her to come down to the station. They had more questions."

"That's nothing to get upset about," Ella said. "The police are searching for Derek's killer. Miranda was his colleague. If there's been a development, it makes sense they'd have more questions for the people close to him."

Ashley discounted Ella's common sense with a vigorous head shake. "But Miranda's lawyer is with her. Why would Miranda need a lawyer for follow-up questions?"

"Did they Mirandize Miranda?" Dotsie asked. She leaned forward, eager for the answer.

Myrtle ignored Dotsie and asked, "She's probably following the lawyer's advice. It's always wise to have a lawyer with you when you're being interviewed by the police, even if you're innocent."

Ashley considered Myrtle's wise advice. "I didn't have a lawyer present when I talked with the police, but I get your point." She turned to me. "So I followed Miranda to the station. I thought I'd wait for her and then we'd stop at the Hearth. But Officer Brody told me the interview would take a while. She all but escorted me out of the building."

"*Interview* is a euphemism for *interrogate*. They spared the professor the perp walk in front of her neighbors." Dotsie crossed her arms across her chest and gave her chin an emphatic bob.

"Dotsie." I pegged her with a stern glance that I knew wouldn't chasten her at all and said to Ashley, "It means nothing."

"No, I agree with her." Ashley nodded at Dotsie. "Why not talk to Miranda at her house if they had only a few questions? Why do it at the station? I know they're going to charge her." Ashley released a fresh burst of tears. Sandy handed her a second cocktail napkin. "Now I'm out another adviser." She blotted her tears, crumpled the two napkins together, and tossed the ball on the coffee table. "My dissertation is cursed. I can't believe this."

"It's not the end of the world," Sandy said. "You'd get another adviser."

Madeline added to the cheer. "The third time's the charm."

"No, it's not." Ashley shifted on the seat to face me. "What did you tell the police?"

"You better not be blaming Veronica for whatever mess Miranda's landed herself in." Sandy's glare matched her sharp tongue.

Ashley turned to Sandy. "Why shouldn't I? She's been playing detective. Veronica's spent more time on campus than the police have. She's talked with the faculty more times than the police have."

"Because they're interviewing *me* for their research projects!" I said, heat filling my cheeks. *Don't blame me if your adviser is in hot water! And I'm sitting here! You don't have to talk about me in the third person.*

"You don't know what the police are doing, Ashley," Sandy said. "You don't know who they've interviewed. The police keep most of their investigation private. They don't share what they've learned with the public. And I'm sure you know that Veronica excels at *playing detective*."

Ella also stepped up to back me. "That's right. Veronica has solved three murder cases. And you don't know how many times the police have interviewed the faculty. They might have brought every member down to the station for a new round of questioning."

"They haven't talked with me twice," Ashley said.

I had an uncharitable thought. *Maybe their questions for Miranda are about you.*

Ashley turned to me, her cheeks flushed and her ire simmering. "You've been hanging around with Susanna too."

I raised my arms in a gesture of surrender. "Call the police! Have them take me down to the station. Throw me into a cell with Miranda." I wondered whether I could withdraw my participation in Ashley's research.

Who knows what she'll write about my mental state? And why should I help her earn her PhD when she's blaming me for her adviser's predicament?

"You should call the police, Veronica. Ashley believes they called Miranda to the station on evidence you gave them. I'm sure Tracey Brody will take your call and update you on the case." Myrtle spoke with authority and an arched-brow look.

"Good idea," I said.

I got up and went into the kitchen. I knew the chance was low that Tracey would take my call. The probability she'd give me information on Miranda's questioning session was even lower. Myrtle had a reason for her suggestion; I wouldn't question it.

My call to Tracey's cell went straight to voice mail. "Hi, Tracey. An unexpected visitor crashed my canasta game. Ashley, and she's sure you've arrested Miranda and thrown away the key. Is this case closed and she has to find yet another adviser?"

For everyone's sake, I hope the third time will be the charm if Ashley does. She and Gretchen can battle to be Bradley's favorite. I didn't rush back to the living room to the canasta group plus one. *Let them talk about the case without me. Ashley can yell about me to her heart's content.*

I stepped onto my back porch and plopped down on the top step. Closing my eyes, I inhaled the cool evening air and relaxed after a few repetitions of conscious breathing. I considered calling Mark to share the surprise twist in the week's canasta gathering, but I decided to wait until I had a full report to give on the night's remaining activity and the outcome of Miranda's visit to the police station. After another minute of enjoying the peace of my backyard, I got up with a groan and crack of my knees.

"You're getting too old for this nonsense, Walsh," I muttered with disgust.

Nonsense. You love it. And fifty-something is the new thirty-whatever. I opened the kitchen's screen door. "Even if you don't look or feel thirty."

The group fell silent when I entered the living room and reclaimed my seat on the couch.

Ashley wore an expression of mild embarrassment. "I'm sorry, Veronica, for barging into your home, for the second time. I'm not usually like this."

"That's okay." I patted her arm. "You've been under a lot of stress."

Ashley let out a mighty sigh. "The year was just so difficult. I had the issue with Derek and was able to switch advisers. I thought everything was going in the right direction and then Derek died, and I'm a suspect. And I don't know why, because the matter between us was resolved to my benefit. Why would I want to hurt Derek now?"

"Really? Some think you wanted to give him a *taste* of his own medicine," Dotsie said. "That you had a *taste* for a measure of revenge to wash the bitter *taste* out of your moth by capitalizing on Derek's *taste* for sweet things. How does that *tas*—"

"Dotsie!" Myrtle, Sandy, Ella, Madeline, and I cried out together. We had become one in our exasperation.

Ella said, "If you're ever curious about the conspiratorial mind, Dotsie's the person to study."

Dotsie glowed with pride.

"Take her away and lock her in observation for a few months," Myrtle suggested.

Dotsie asked, "What would you do for a partner?"

"Maybe Ashley would like to join us," Myrtle said.

"Join you in what?" Ashley asked. "Are you some sort of a club."

"Canasta!" Madeline said.

"Neat." Ashley stood, ready to make her exit. "My grandmother plays canasta at her senior center."

My fifty is thirty became fifty is thirty plus fifty.

On that discourteous end note, I escorted Ashley to the door and returned to the living room. "So who said what that made Ashley apologize?"

"First, what did Tracey Brody say?" Myrtle asked. 'You *did* call her?"

"Yes, and she didn't answer. She's probably grilling Miranda right this minute."

"My psychological diagnosis is Ashley is prone to fits of hyperbole and hysteria."

We all laughed at Myrtle's quip.

Sandy offered details on what went down in the living room during my brief sojourn to the kitchen and backyard. "I told her she was way out of line stomping over here and making a wild accusation against you. Myrtle said her behavior was very unprofessional and Ella added immature. Madeline reminded Ashley of how you've risked your life doing your civic duty for Barton and Dotsie said Ashley was lucky she hasn't been arrested and said she was still on the suspect list."

"I scared her by suggesting the police might not suspect Miranda at all," Dotsie said. "I put it in her head it might all be a setup to see how *she* reacted. The police could be interviewing Miranda about Ashley and her motive and opportunity to poison Derek."

"That's some serious head game." The idea of Dotsie spinning a theory to intimidate Ashley made me feel a bit of snarky amusement.

Dotsie continued. "Maybe the entire department participated in the poisoning, a la *Murder on the Orient Express*!"

"That's nuts, Dotsie," Myrtle said.

"No way would they do that," I said. "They had the usual disagreements with Derek, but no one hated him. They wouldn't team up to kill him."

Dotsie clung to her theory. "They may've teamed up to make him spend the night hanging over the toilet, puking his guts out. A dose of misery for the misery he's caused others."

"On that lovely note, shall we get to the canasta?" Sandy said.

The ladies filed into the dining room. "I'll carry that," I said to Dotsie, who was making a move to lift the chair Sandy had brought from the dining table.

"It's a good thing you hosted this week," she said. "Otherwise, we would have missed all this to-do."

For all the grief the "to-do" had caused, I agreed with Dotsie.

And as nutty as her theory was, I couldn't help but cast Barton's version of *Murder on the Orient Express* while I cleaned up after the ladies left. Kyle played the distractor, keeping Derek in his office. Miranda was the guard, standing watch in the hall. Ashley opened the soda bottle and held a funnel while Gretchen poured the antifreeze into the soda. Did others stay in their offices, playing dumb?

I shook my head and turned off the hall light. "You're nuts," I muttered on the way up the stairs to my bedroom.

Chapter Thirty-Three

Tracey returned my call the next morning. "Be in the alley in five minutes."

I was. Tracey's cruiser was parked facing the Sycamore Street entrance to the alley. I hopped in the front seat, but before I could say more than "hi," Tracey told me to buckle my seat belt. Once I did, she put the cruiser in *Drive* and pulled out of the alley.

"Where are we going?"

"Your house. This will take more than a few minutes. I figured I'd get a free cup of coffee out of it."

"You got it."

"Ashley is certainly dedicated to her professor. She made quite a scene at the station."

"At my house too. But it's not about her dedication to Miranda," I said. "Ashley's freaked out about the effect Miranda's arrest will have on her dissertation."

"Can't blame her. She had a contentious relationship with her first adviser, and now her second adviser might be facing prosecution for murdering the first mentor," Tracey said.

She parked in front of my house and we went inside. I made us each a cup of coffee and sat across from her at the kitchen table.

"So, what about Miranda? Have you charged her?"

"No. And don't assume we will."

"So why did you call her to the station?"

Tracey blew a few cooling puffs across her black, sugar-free coffee and took a sip of it. "We had more questions." She set the mug on the table.

"What prompted these questions? Come on, work with me. You got your free cup of coffee."

Tracey took three sips of that free coffee.

Is she reconsidering whatever she was going to tell me? Or did she get tired of buying coffee and decided she'd take advantage of my hospitality and eagerness for information on the case?

"Remember, this is confidential," Tracey said. "Miranda applied for a job in the dean's office. Associate Dean of Undergraduate Studies. Derek didn't recommend her for the promotion. He told the dean that she was an excellent professor, but she didn't have the administrative experience for the job. He also said that Miranda was a self-promoter, more interested in her own career than in applying herself to her responsibilities to the students and Arden."

I take back the doubt and accusation. Tracey just needed caffeine.

"That stings. And Miranda knew that he'd said that? Did Derek tell her?" *If Derek had told her, Miranda would be an excellent actress indeed. Her cheerful demeanor at his party, her eulogy. She sure did act as if she respected and liked him.*

"She claims she didn't know that he didn't support her for the promotion," Tracey said. "But she's well aware of the lackluster annual performance review Derek gave her."

"Arden let you read the review?" I asked.

Tracey sampled her coffee. "We found the reviews for all the psychology faculty on Derek's work laptop."

"And..."

"He gave her a good review for teaching and advising, but wrote that the quality of her research could be better, and that she should do more service for the program and Arden and less advancing of her own career."

"Similar to the remarks he made to the dean."

"Yeah. They'd met the Thursday before he died and discussed

the review."

This is getting interesting. "Had Derek submitted the review?"

"No," Tracey said.

"Did you get a look at the review he gave Miranda last year?"

"Yeah. Derek was more generous with his praise in the teaching, research, and service categories."

"Hmm." I thought for a moment while Tracey enjoyed her coffee. "Was he angry because she had challenged him over the situation with Ashley or did he sabotage her chance for the assistant dean's position because he was jealous she was under consideration and he wasn't?"

"Either or both could be possible."

"What about the reviews for the other faculty?"

Tracey shook her head. "Nothing that would provide a motive."

"Did you find anything else on the laptop that is relevant?"

"It was turned on the evening after Derek died."

"By Miranda?"

Tracey nodded. "Derek had brought the laptop home on Monday. When Miranda visited Susanna on Tuesday, Susanna gave her the laptop to return to the department."

"Oh. So..."

"Miranda claims that she only wanted to see if the laptop contained department business that she needed to know immediately."

I snickered at Tracey's ironic delivery. "But she couldn't get past Derek's password."

"Nope."

"If Miranda had deleted the review from Derek's laptop, would your forensic people have been able to retrieve it?" I asked. "From the recycle bin if Miranda forgot to empty it or from the depths of the hard drive if she did?"

"Yes. We have our ways." Tracey winked. "There'd also be the copy of the review attached to the email Derek sent Miranda. That would be on the college's email server, even if she was able to get into his email and delete it."

"I wonder if there's anything else Miranda wanted to delete. Or read."

"Still to be determined. Miranda asked whether all of Derek's files would remain intact and the laptop returned to the department. She's concerned that Derek had private information in his files. Personal info on his research subjects. She didn't want it *out there*."

"No, she wanted all that information for herself. Miranda wanted to take all the research Derek was working on and publish it under her own name!"

Tracey laughed at my Eureka! expression. "This is why I tell you more than I should. You're comedy gold."

I soaked up the admiration and then told Tracey of my second session with Miranda. "She wants me to recruit my friends for her article."

Tracey laughed. "I admire her boldness."

"I admit, I do too. I like her. Is all the evidence you have against her circumstantial?"

"Yep. Including this last piece. Miranda was the first person to arrive at the office the day Derek was poisoned."

"She admitted that?"

"No. She arrived at seven forty-five, before the building was unlocked at eight. She had to use her faculty badge to get in and that swipe was logged into campus security's database. No one else from the psychology staff used their badge to enter."

"I guess Miranda wasn't caught on a surveillance camera carrying a bag from the Food Mart?"

"With a soda bottle protruding from it?" Tracey asked. "No. All she carried was her big tote bag."

"Which could certainly conceal a liter bottle of black cherry soda. Did anyone else who worked in the building arrive before eight?"

"Noelle Lopez and a professor and admin from Art History. They've been interviewed." Tracey finished her coffee and stood. "Remember, this is all confidential. Not to be discussed with anyone. Except Professor Burke. Because I know you'll tell him no matter what I say." She tossed me a grin and rinsed her mug and put it in the dishwasher.

"That's right. Don't worry. I won't make any Freudian slips."

I kept my word and played dumb through the inquiring phone calls I received from the canasta ladies. Nor did I confer with Carol or Claire, and I didn't call Mark to share the details. I'd tell him when I saw him.

Instead, I went about the business of All Things and, in the moments I wasn't assisting a customer or talking with my staff, contemplated the facts Tracey had laid out.

Those facts formed a case against Miranda. They showed a motive and a fifteen-minute window—at least—of opportunity. The means—antifreeze—was easy to obtain and dispose of without raising anyone's suspicions.

"It's all too neat," I mumbled. It was a few minutes before noon and I was in the shop's Christmas corner, which we kept stocked with ornaments and holiday-themed items year-round. Many visitors to Barton, particularly those who came to the Adirondacks for their summer vacations, liked to bring home an ornament or two to remember their holiday in the mountains. But from January to October, the corner was a fairly quiet place to think or catch a moment's peace.

Would Miranda really kill Derek over a poor performance review? I moved a skiing Santa ornament from the back of the tree to the front. *Or would she have pushed harder to succeed and flaunt it in Derek's face?* That seemed more like the Miranda I had gotten to know.

To Miranda, living well and flaunting it in front of Derek every chance she got would've been the best revenge.

"If I'm right..."

Someone else thought revenge was best served cold, straight from the bottle.

Chapter Thirty-Four

Miranda came into the shop mid-afternoon. She carried a shopping bag from my mother's bookstore. "A bit of retail therapy. Your mother is delightful."

"And you've come to All Things for additional therapy?" I asked, joking but not joking.

"We have some beautiful new pieces of blown glass, made by local artist Lisette Rosen," Claire said from behind the counter.

I turned so Miranda couldn't see my face and offered Claire a wink of approval. The blown-glass items are among the shop's most expensive stock.

"I'm here to talk with you, Veronica. Do you have a few minutes?"

"I do."

"In private?" Miranda asked.

Claire gave a soft click of her tongue. I looked over my shoulder and met her gaze. She offered me the blasé smile of someone who doesn't care they've been caught in the act of doing something they shouldn't be doing. Like eating the inventory. Or eavesdropping on your boss's conversation.

"Go ahead." Claire fluttered her fingers in a gesture toward the door.

"Ashley told me about her visit to your home last night." Miranda rounded the corner of the building and moved close to the shop's side window that overlooked Sycamore Street.

"Ashley made quite a dramatic entrance and presentation. Her loyalty to you is impressive."

"And I appreciate it. I would have liked to have kept my visit with the Barton police private, but Ashley panicked and ran to you." Miranda's glance turned stern. "I trust your discretion and I hope your friends will have the same respect for my privacy."

Maybe I should invite Miranda to our next game. She'd fit in well. She and Dotsie would be fast friends.

"Well..."

"Thanks to Ashley's indiscretion, I need to do a bit of clean up." Miranda fixed her stare on me. "I *didn't* poison Derek. The police haven't cleared me yet, but I am innocent. I don't want to be included in your detective work. Don't try to find supporting evidence against me, because there is none."

"Then why did the police question you?"

Let's see how much she tells me and if it matches what Tracey said.

Miranda let out a weary sigh. "I visited Susanna the day after Derek died. She gave me his laptop to return to the department. I tried to log onto it, *just* to see if there was any important department information I needed to have before I turned it in."

"That's nothing to raise suspicions—"

"The police think I was trying to delete the poor performance review Derek gave me so no one else would see it." Miranda moved her glance to the bridal salon on the opposite corner. "I didn't poison Derek over a bad performance review. Look, I've had tenure for seven years. I deserve to be promoted to full professor, but Derek didn't agree. We'd argued about it several times. He wouldn't nominate me for the promotion or support it. I think he didn't want me to get the promotion faster than he did."

"How long did it take him?"

"Ten years."

"What about male professors who wanted a promotion?"

"Only one has been in the position to become full since I've been tenured," Miranda said. "He was promoted to full professor in seven years. Derek wasn't the department chair at the time."

"I'm sorry."

"Thanks."

I hesitated before asking, "Do you think Derek opposed you because you're a woman?"

"I think so. I didn't kill him. I wanted Derek around so when I did get the promotion, I could shove it in his face."

"Good plan."

Miranda's cell rang. "Excuse me." She reached into her purse to retrieve the phone. "Hi, Bradley." She took a few paces down Sycamore.

To give her privacy, I moved around the corner and stood by the front window, watching the traffic pass and thinking about what Miranda said.

Was she playing a mind game with me? Did she indulge me with compliments about my discretion and detecting skills to soften me toward her defense? Did she think coming to me and presenting her case would incline me to believe her?

I did believe Miranda, particularly her declaration that she wanted to flaunt her success to Derek. He was an obstacle to her promotion. She wanted to earn it despite his obstructions, not achieve it by removing him from her path.

Miranda came around the corner. A scowl had replaced her determined countenance.

"Is everything all right?"

She clenched her jaw. "I can't get a full professorship, but a plagiarist was just given tenure!"

"What? Who—"

Miranda jerked her head toward the corner. We returned to the shop's side window.

"I trust you will keep this information to yourself." Miranda spoke *sotto voce*, though no one was within earshot.

"Absolutely."

"Bradley was accused of plagiarism last September. One of the external reviewers for his tenure—do you know about the external review process?"

"Yes. Mark recently told me. He's going to do a review this summer."

"I hope he doesn't find the candidate plagiarized his work or someone else's. That's what one of Bradley's reviewers discovered."

"Bradley plagiarized the reviewer's work?"

"No. He didn't give proper attribution to another psychologist's research in a book he wrote a few years ago. He included three passages from a book without citing them. Without the credit, readers would think he had conducted the study."

"I bet Bradley said it was a mistake."

"Of course that's what he claimed. He was sloppy."

"A case of cryptomnesia," I said, pleased by both the chance to show off my knowledge and Miranda's stunned look. "Noelle told me about how every year PhD candidates who apply for the Instructor Prize unconsciously rip off the topic of a professor's course."

"Unconscious, so they say."

"Did Arden conduct an investigation?"

"Yes. A very quiet investigation. Only a few of us in the department know of the accusation. I think the powers that be decided before the investigation even began that Bradley would get tenure."

"Even if the investigation proved he intentionally plagiarized the work?"

"That's why they kept it quiet. Bradley's the golden boy. The administration loves his glossy media presence. He brings prestige to the college. The investigation concluded he'd made a mistake."

Miranda's attitude was all sour lemons. I felt a bit that way myself. "That stinks."

"That's modern academia."

"What do your colleagues think?"

Miranda gave a half shrug. "Some believed Bradley. It is easy to make such a mistake with all the information we have collected for an article or book. But it's not excusable! We're professionals. We have to be diligent and give credit to our peers for their work. We each expect the same."

"What did Derek think?"

"He gave Bradley the benefit of the doubt." Miranda's resentful attitude deepened. "He supported the male plagiarist but not an honest, hardworking female colleague."

"I'm sorry."

"Thanks. I don't mean to unload my frustration on you." Miranda started for Orchard Street.

"The irony of all this isn't lost on me. I'm innocent yet I'm dragged to police headquarters and interrogated in the poisoning of my department's chair while my colleague, who's guilty of plagiarism, is given a lifetime appointment. Thanks for listening, Veronica." She gave my elbow a squeeze, bounded up the sidewalk to the next corner, and dashed across Orchard to where her car was parked.

Her hyperbole wasn't lost on me. *Dragged to police headquarter. Interrogated. Guilty of plagiarism.*

Perhaps Bradley had made an awful mistake and deserved tenure. Or perhaps he'd gotten away with plagiarism. If he had, I hoped he'd be hypervigilant about giving proper attribution in his future articles and books.

"What was that about?" Claire asked when I entered the shop.

"She wanted to arrange another interview for her research project."

"Miranda's expression was rather intense. She must be very passionate about her research."

"She is."

Claire and I locked glances for a moment.

"Mm-hmm." Claire breezed by me. "You are the soul of discretion."

That I am.

Chapter Thirty-Five

The walk home from All Things gave me a few distraction-free minutes to contemplate what Miranda had said.

Derek's acceptance of Bradley's claim that the plagiarism was an innocent error surprised me. Bradley was an example of the modern psychologist Derek lamented in our conversation in his living room: an academic wading in the shallow end of the research pool. Miranda's description of his "glossy media presence" was apt.

Maybe I'm wrong to assume that Derek didn't support Gretchen's proposed class for the Instructor Prize because it was too similar to Bradley's current course offering. Because if that's the reason he didn't recommend her class, why would he support a more consequential act of imitation?

Was the benefit of the doubt Derek extended to Bradley a cover for a covert move against the young professor?

"Tell me about how external reviewers are selected for a tenure candidate," I asked Mark twenty minutes later. Does the department chair select them?"

"They'll recommend one or two reviewers." Mark took a sip of his soda and set the glass on the table between us. We were in our usual seats by the fire pit.

"And you said before that five or six professors are asked to do a review."

"Yes. A department committee will draw up a list and the candidate will offer a few names. No one he or she has worked with, been a student of, or has more than a passing acquaintance with can be selected to give a review."

"So no one who would have a subjective view of the candidate's work or a personal relationship with the candidate?"

"Correct. The candidate will be shown the committee's list and will be allowed to strike off names of anyone with whom he has a personal history. After that, several people are chosen to be invited to review the candidate."

"Who contacts the reviewers?"

"The chairperson will make the initial contact and, if the invitation is accepted, will send out the materials for review."

I shifted in my chair. "If the chairperson wanted a certain person to review a candidate, he could nominate the person. And if that person wasn't one of the few selected to review, the chairperson could invite him or her to review without the committee knowing?"

"I suppose." Mark's studious gaze held mine. "Where are you going with these questions?"

"The psychology department has been sitting on a big secret since last fall. An external reviewer accused Bradley of plagiarism."

Mark's expression darkened. "How'd you learn this?"

"Miranda came by the shop this afternoon." I gave Mark a quick summary of why the police had questioned her. "While we were talking, Bradley called with the news that he'd been given tenure. Miranda's furious that he was given tenure despite the plagiarism charge and she's struggling to get a promotion to full professor."

"Did Bradley defend himself against the charge?"

"He insisted it was a sloppy mistake. The committee that investigated the case agreed."

"Huh." Mark stared at the line of spruces at the back of my yard.

"How would you feel if this happened in your department? If one of your colleagues was guilty of plagiarism?"

"It's an easy mistake to make and we professors take great care not to make that error. Bradley could be lying to cover himself. Or he could be telling the truth."

"If you were on the committee deciding his tenure, would you vote to give it to him?"

"I can't answer a hypothetical question. I'd have to look through his material, see the specifics of the plagiarism charge, and hear the case for and against him. I'm not happy the charge was kept quiet."

"Miranda believes Bradley was protected because of his burgeoning media stardom. He brings prestige to Arden."

Mark was silent.

I waited a few seconds and then continued. "She also said that Derek gave Bradley the benefit of the doubt on the plagiarism charge."

Mark twisted in his chair to face me. "He did?"

"Yeah. And I'm shocked. I'd think that Derek would be against Bradley getting tenure."

Mark's brows knit together and rose. "Derek may've advocated against tenure in private but supported Bradley in public on the chance that Bradley was given tenure. They'd be colleagues for a long time. Derek wouldn't want Bradley to be an adversary. He'd want to have a decent working relationship with him."

"Yet Derek didn't support Miranda for full professor. He didn't seem to care about his working relationship with her."

"Maybe we should give Derek the benefit of the doubt on that and believe it was because of his ten-year policy, not because of Miranda's gender or ethnicity. Where are you going with all this?"

I grinned. "Would you give me a C grade if I were a student and had taken so long to get to the point?"

"I'd take another half-grade off for delaying and not answering my question." Mark returned the smile and took a mouthful of cola.

"What if Derek's benefit of the doubt wasn't to cover himself if Bradley became a lifetime member of the psychology department but a shield to conceal his role in the plagiarism charge?" I asked.

"And what do you have to support that theory?"

"Nothing. Yet. But here's the rest of the theory. Derek

discovered that Bradley had plagiarized and, instead of exposing it himself, put into position someone who would recognize the copied passages and make the charge?"

"What would be Derek's motive?"

"He didn't like the direction colleagues and contemporaries were taking in their research. He believed some were doing research for their own gain and acclaim and not for the benefit of society. With his growing fame, I think Bradley was one of the colleagues Derek disdained. I think, despite the disdain, he was also jealous of the attention Bradley's research received. The lectures featured on social media channels, deals with news networks to be an expert analyst, etcetera." I paused for a breath. "He didn't want Susanna to collaborate with Eric. If he was jealous of his wife's greater success, he'd be jealous of a colleague, particularly a younger, handsome professor whose career would soon eclipse Derek's."

Mark set down his glass and shifted his weight to the edge of his chair. "So Derek chose an external reviewer who would recognize the stolen passages and report it in their review with the hope Bradley wouldn't get tenure?"

"And Bradley figured out Derek set him up and poisoned his black cherry soda!"

"Okay." Mark's short, calm response was maddening. "Prove it. What's your plan? The reviewer statements are confidential."

"I'll ask Miranda whose work Bradley plagiarized. The names of the reviewers aren't confidential, are they?"

"No, but—"

"Miranda will tell me because I'll be helping prove her innocence. She'll trust me with the information."

Is that a smirk or a look of pride Mark's giving me?

"All right. How will you prove that Derek knew Bradley had plagiarized another psychologist's work?"

"If Derek selected the reviewer who charged—"

"Anonymously, remember."

"If Derek selected the reviewer, that would be the first step."

"Was it the reviewer's work Bradley plagiarized? Did Miranda say?" Mark asked.

"No. It was someone else's."

"So you have to prove Derek knew that person's work and knew the reviewer knew that person's work well enough that he or she would recognize the passages."

"Not impossible," I said. I maintained a firm grip on my theory, despite the shots Mark took at it.

Possible." Mark took a pause. "The reviewer could have edited a book that included the passages Bradley stole. Or they collaborated on a research study or book."

"So, again, not impossible."

"No. Get a good night's rest. You have a difficult assignment to complete tomorrow." Mark tipped his glass against my glass of ginger ale.

Proving my theory would be a challenge, but I was confident that I'd succeed. Revenge against a person who attempted to destroy a high-profile career was a strong motive for murder.

"Will I get an A-plus if I complete the assignment?"

"You'll get a top grade, a permanent place on the dean's list, and earn your PhD in one fell swoop if you prove Bradley's the poisoner."

"And an honorary degree from Arden? It's the least your college can give me if I solve their professor's murder."

"I'll start the campaign immediately."

Chapter Thirty-Six

"Whose work was Bradley accused of plagiarizing?" I asked Miranda in a phone call the next morning.

"Sylvia Taub's. From her book, *The Lifespan of the Human Mind.*"

"Will you give me the names of the professors who reviewed Bradley for tenure?"

Miranda was silent.

Uh oh. Is she going to tell me it's none of my business? That she doesn't have access to the list? What if the names are on Derek's laptop and no one in the department has a hard copy! Panic settled over me.

"Do you need it for your investigation?" she finally asked.

"Yes."

"I can get you the names."

"Can you tell me which reviewer Derek selected?"

Miranda said, "I think I can."

"Any chance you can find out which reviewer exposed Bradley's plagiarism?"

"I think so."

"You won't get into trouble—"

"I am the acting head of the department, Veronica. I have the authority." Miranda's tone was more matter-of-fact than peeved at the suggestion she may not have the authority to gather the information.

"Thanks, Miranda."

Miranda called me back in thirty minutes. "Here are the names of Bradley's tenure reviewers." She gave me six names, pausing after each so I could write the name on a notepad. "I'm certain Derek selected Herbert McTigue."

"This is a great start. Thank you."

I tossed my phone aside and typed McTigue's and Taub's names into my Internet search engine.

"Wow!"

McTigue and Taub had collaborated on three books and Taub was a contributor to a textbook McTigue had edited. The textbook had a bold orange stripe in its cover design.

"*That* book was on Derek's bookshelf! I packed that book!"

If the evidence was in my hands...

I called Miranda. "Time for me to invite you to lunch. My house, twelve-thirty?"

At the stroke of twelve-thirty, I welcomed Miranda into my home. "Explain your need for the external reviewers' names," she asked with urgency. A large brown envelope, the kind businesses use for intra-office mail, stuck out from her tote bag.

I led her down the short hallway and into my dining room. I'd set the table for lunch but had left the cold cuts and salads in the refrigerator. Miranda and I sat across from each other.

"Derek knew Bradley plagiarized Sylvia Taub's work and intentionally selected McTigue to do a tenure review because he knew McTigue would expose Bradley."

Miranda crossed her arms on the table and leaned forward. "Connect these dots for me."

"I believe Derek was jealous of Bradley's growing profile in the media."

"I agree." Miranda kept her gaze steady on me.

I was thankful she didn't patronize me and say "You don't need a PhD to figure that out" or "A first grader could tell you that."

"He was jealous of your career and Susanna's too. He tried to hold both of you back and I think he attempted to sabotage Bradley's career." I took a breath and presented my findings of the morning. "McTigue and Taub co-authored three books. And McTigue edited a book that Taub contributed to. I'm certain I saw that book in Derek's home office last week when I helped Susanna pack up his books. More important than that, Bradley may've been in Derek's office the day of the barbecue." I gave Miranda a quick account of my conversation with Bradley in Derek and Susanna's front hall. "If he saw the book..."

We were quiet for a few seconds. Miranda's expression moved from pensive to a tight jaw to a wicked scowl.

"That S.O.B!" She banged the table with her fist. "I'm going to kill Bradley!" Miranda bolted to her feet.

I scrambled from my chair and blocked her path to the front door. "Wait!"

"Why?"

"We need to confirm Derek had the book in his home office and then give it and the theory to the police."

"Then off we go to Susanna's. I'll drive."

My stomach grumbled. So much for lunch.

"What a perfect plan." Miranda steered her car through the streets that lay between my house and Susanna's. She did exceed the speed limit but not by so much that one of Barton's finest would pull her over for speeding. Her monologue kept me from imagining the reason she'd give the police officer.

"No one made the connection between McTigue and Taub when the plagiarism charge was made. Derek must have used the textbook in one of his classes. Did you notice if he was a contributor too?"

"I didn't look."

"Never mind. We'll know soon enough."

"Was Bradley in the office today?" I asked.

"Yes. He received many congratulations on his tenure victory." Miranda clicked her tongue. "A woman wouldn't have been given the benefit of the doubt."

"What would've happened if Bradley wasn't given tenure? Would he have left Arden immediately?"

Miranda turned onto Susanna's street. "He would've been allowed to stay on staff for a year while he sought a position elsewhere."

"Would he have been able to get another teaching job?"

"Yeah, he would find a place at a lower-tier university." Miranda pulled to a stop in front of Susanna's house. "Let's get this proof."

Susanna welcomed us with a puzzled look. "What's going on? Has something happened?" Her querying glance fixed on Miranda.

Miranda took charge with a demanding "Do you still have the boxes of Derek's books you and Veronica packed last week?"

"Yes. They're still in his office."

Miranda brushed past Susanna and charged down the hall into the office with me close on her heels. The boxes were set on the desk and on the floor under the street-facing window.

I opened the flaps of one of the boxes on the desk and took the books out, two at a time. Miranda began a search through the boxes on the floor.

Susanna stood in the doorway. "What are you looking for? Veronica, did you lose a ring or an earring?"

"No. She's solved the case. Veronica knows who killed Derek." Miranda, kneeling on the floor, made fast work of going through the boxes. She dropped each book on the floor; the sight conjured the image of children on Christmas morning tossing over their shoulders every gift that wasn't a toy.

I paused my search and turned to Susanna. "Did Derek tell you that Bradley was accused of plagiarism?"

Susanna's confusion deepened. "What? No."

Miranda gave her the details of the accusation and gave me the responsibility of telling Susanna her husband may have choreographed the revelation. "At your party, Derek and I had a conversation about our careers and the current state of our professions. In retrospect, I have the impression he didn't respect Bradley's work."

"You're right. Derek didn't respect the celebrity some psychologists enjoy. He thought it compromised their research." Susanna came over to the desk and leaned her back against the unopened boxes. "He believed they tailored their research to a media audience."

"I think he chose McTigue to review Bradley's tenure dossier, knowing he'd recognize Taub's unattributed passages in the book Bradley wrote." I took the last two books from the box, set them on the stack I'd built, and tossed the empty box into a corner. "Do you think Derek—"

Susanna finished. "Would do that? Yes."

Miranda opened a second box. "And Veronica thinks, and I agree, that Bradley saw the book in Derek's library the day of your barbecue, figured out it was Derek who tried to sabotage his tenure, and poisoned the soda Derek kept in the department's pantry."

Susanna's reaction wasn't immediate. She looked from Miranda to me, her eyes wide and her mouth agape. "That bastard!" She turned and ripped open the box on the end of the desk. "What are we looking for?"

"Anything by McTigue or Taub. The book I remember seeing here was white with a wide orange stripe. A textbook edited by McTigue." I moved the box next to Susanna's to create a space on the desk for both of us to stack books.

We worked in tense silence for a minute.

"I found it!!" Miranda rose to her full height, the McTigue book raised above her head. She moved to the desk and stood between Susanna and me. Miranda placed the book on the pile we'd built and opened it to the index. She found Taub's name and thumbed to the pages on which her work was mentioned. On the first page Miranda flipped to was a highlighted passage. Someone—I assumed Derek—had drawn a yellow square around the several lines.

"This is an attributed passage from Taub's research. Hold the place." Miranda handed me the open book, crossed to the window to retrieve the intra-office envelope from her tote, and re-claimed the book.

She lay the opened textbook across the stack of books, whipped several sheets of paper from the envelope, riffled through them, and pulled out one sheet. She checked the page against the book's highlighted passage.

"Here it is! This is one of the passages Bradley lifted from Taub's research." Miranda referred to McTigue's index, checked a couple of unmarked pages, and flipped forward a few pages to another passage highlighted in yellow.

Miranda slipped another sheet from the envelope and compared it to the highlighted text. "Yep. The second passage Bradley didn't attribute to Taub. Sloppy." She finished with a mild expletive.

She located the third highlighted—and plagiarized—passage in the book. "Here's proof Derek knew Bradley plagiarized Taub and chose McTigue to expose him." Miranda's glower was fierce. She closed the textbook with a loud clap. "Time for a visit to Arden's newest hire. This will be the shortest tenure in history."

From the near distance came the slam of a car door. I figured it came from a neighbor's driveway, perhaps Vicki returning home from work.

I grabbed the book from Miranda and snatched up the dossier pages. "We need to convince the police first. Leave the visit to them."

Miranda's frown was more fearsome than her glare. "I don't like anti-climac—"

The chime of the doorbell startled us all.

I turned to Susanna. "Are you expecting company?"

"Yes." Her cheeks blanched. "Bradley."

Chapter Thirty-Seven

Miranda spoke in a whisper. "Bradley couldn't know that I pulled his dossier. I was very careful. I consulted with Noelle on who selected each reviewer. I told her not to say anything—"

"Bradley's here to pick up the books," Susanna said, her expression taut with worry. "Remember, Veronica, when we went to campus last week—"

"He offered to collect the books. I bet he couldn't wait to get his hands on this particular book." I loosened my grip on McTigue's textbook. *Bradley's fingerprints might be on it!*

The doorbell rang again.

"This book isn't going anywhere. It's evidence!" Miranda snatched the textbook from my grasp. "Don't keep your guest waiting."

"Don't smear the fingerprints on that book! And don't anybody say anything." *Do you really believe Susanna or Miranda are going to listen to you?* "I'm calling the police." I yanked my cell from my pocket and called Tracey. "Thank goodness you answered!"

Susanna strode into the hall. "Coming!"

I went to the corner of Derek's office, out of view from the hallway, and spoke to Tracey in a low voice. "I'm at Susanna's house. Come now! But no sirens. I think we've solved the murder."

Miranda wrested the phone from my hand. "Don't end this call. Listen to our conversation. I will get you a confession."

Good grief.

Miranda put the call on speakerphone and muted it. "Bradley

won't admit anything to the police. This is all circumstantial evidence. But I know how to push his buttons." She stuffed the dossier papers into the envelope and tucked it and McTigue's book in the desk drawer. Still clutching my cell, she moved to the open window that overlooked the front lawn. "This is perfect. The police will overhear everything," she whispered.

I noted the glimmer in her eyes before she turned and left the room. "All right, since you're in charge, why don't I go home and eat the lunch I bought for you?" I muttered.

I followed her down the hall. Susanna and Bradley were in the living room.

"I was telling Bradley that you two were here for lunch." I marveled at Susanna's calm delivery.

Who's the Emmy-winning actress here? Geez, these professors can put on a good act.

"Congratulations on your tenure, Bradley," I said. "I hope you have big plans to celebrate your achievement."

"I'll go out with some friends. I'll celebrate with my family when we're all together in July. We'll do something special then, I'm sure." Bradley's cheeks glowed with pleasure in his victory.

"We'll plan a department celebration for next week. Maybe dinner." Miranda offered Bradley a toothy smile.

"Let's do that. I'm grateful to everyone in the department for the support you've given me. Not only this past year but my entire time at Arden."

"Of course we'd support you. You're a valued member of the faculty." Miranda moved to the center of the living room and stood facing the window to the street.

"My happiness is diminished by Derek's absence," Bradley said to Susanna. "He was remarkable, an invaluable mentor. I wish he were here to share this moment. I hope you'll come to our celebration."

"I'll be there." Susanna's reply lacked enthusiasm, though she offered Bradley a faint smile.

Miranda moved to the mantel and ran her finger down the Washington bust. "Bradley, I hope I have your vote to head the department." She stroked the Freud bust and moved the Lincoln bust a half-inch closer to Freud.

She's stalling until Tracey arrives. I admired Miranda's poise, though I wasn't sure if I was happy about her stealing my sleuthing thunder. I was the one who solved the case, after all. *And wanted to avoid this scene with Bradley. Can't do anything about it now.* I'd cede the stage to Miranda, let her be the ham eating the scenery. *And if this scene goes sideways, I'll make sure Chief Price knows Miranda was the director on the set.*

"I was thinking I might throw my hat in the ring for the seat."

Miranda shot a scowl at Bradley in the pause that followed his announcement.

He chuckled. "Joking. You deserve to be the chairperson, Miranda. I don't think anyone will challenge you."

Miranda's glower lingered. She shifted her glance to the window. After a moment, her lips set into a relaxed line and she stepped away from the mantel. "Susanna said that you're here to pick up Derek's books."

"Yes." Bradley's gaze tracked Miranda's steps across the room. "I'm going to bring the books to the office so staff and students can take what they want. I thought I'd arranged them on the conference room table—"

"Great idea."

Miranda went into the hallway. Susanna, Bradley, and I were obliged to follow.

Miranda struck a pose before the framed print. "This painting fascinates me. Great title. *Not to Be Reproduced.* You see that book, Bradley?" She pointed at the Poe book in the painting.

"Yeah."

"One of the themes of that book is plagiarism. Isn't that interesting?"

"Uh-huh." His glance moved to the boxes of books.

Miranda's gaze tracked his. "Veronica and I just took a look through the books. And we ended up making a mess of Susanna's work." She led us into Derek's office. "Veronica selected a few books. One on how to tell when someone is lying. Another on body language and a text on the criminal mind. They should assist her in future detective cases, though I certainly hope there are no more murders in Barton she'll have to solve."

"I second that," Bradley said.

Miranda stood by the desk, set my phone on the corner, and took a dramatic turn to face us. "It won't take the four of us long to re-pack the books. Have you selected all the books you'd like?" Bradley looked from Miranda to me. He bent over the stack of books on the floor under the window. "Sure you don't want this book on juvenile delinquency, Veronica?" He laughed and tossed the book in the box.

"No, thanks. I don't investigate minors."

Miranda watched Bradley stack a few of the books in a box before she opened the desk drawer and withdrew the McTigue book. "Are there any particular texts you'd like? I understand you had a good look at the shelves the day of the party."

Bradley's glance darted from Miranda to McTigue's book. "Nothing in particular."

"Really? What about this book?"

Bradley showed no reaction. He moved closer and squinted. "I'll leave textbooks for the students."

Miranda made a show of flipping through the book's pages. "It's interesting that the only highlighted sections in this book are the passages you plagiarized from Sylvia Taub's work. *Not to be reproduced* is a lesson you didn't learn in grad school."

Bradley shrugged. No nervous twitches, blinks, or coughs.

I felt a tinge of panic; had I come to the wrong conclusion and convinced a vulnerable Susanna and peeved Miranda it was correct? Was I so eager to solve the murder that I'd spun a few facts into a tale of fiction?

"About the tenure celebration." Miranda stepped a few paces from the desk and turned to face Bradley. "You'll have to let us know how many visitors you're allowed at one time in your jail cell. But don't expect a file to be baked in the cake."

"What are you talking about? Is this a joke?" Bradley chuckled and cocked his head.

Miranda, her cool demeanor still in place, said, "No. No joke. You—"

"Killed my husband."

Bradley, still appearing unperturbed, took a step toward Susanna. "Susanna, I—"

"Put poison in Derek's soda," Susanna said, "because he deliberately chose a reviewer who would expose your plagiarism."

"I didn't plagiarize Taub! It was a careless mistake!"

It's interesting Bradley's more upset about a plagiarism accusation than a charge of murder.

"The tenure committee obviously thought so." Miranda dropped the book on the desk. "Lucky you. But you wanted revenge. Derek almost ruined your career. I wonder if he had a Plan B in case you won tenure. Would he have anonymously leaked the accusation to the press? The *New York Times*, perhaps?"

"You're all talking nonsense."

"No, we're not. You poisoned..." Though her voice faltered, Susanna maintained her composure. "You poisoned Derek. *You* killed my husband."

"This is absurd." Bradley drew close to Susanna and moved to place his hand on her shoulder.

She slapped his hand away and stepped back. "Don't touch me."

Bradley turned an accusatory look on me. "What have you been telling these two? What stories have you spun playing *detective*?"

He took a step toward me. I prepared to defend myself, but Susanna stepped between us before I or Bradley could land a blow.

"Admit it, Bradley," Susanna said, "you figured out it was McTigue who exposed you and that it was Derek who chose him to review your dossier after you saw that book—" Susanna pointed to the textbook, "on that shelf." She gestured to the empty bookcase.

Bradley's shoulders sagged. "It was a mistake."

"The plagiarism, I assume you mean," Miranda said. "Because pouring antifreeze into someone's soda bottle isn't a move one makes by accident."

"Shut up, Miranda." Bradley clenched his teeth and regarded each of us in turn. "You can't prove anything."

"We already have," I said. "Did you switch out a poisoned bottle for the one Derek—"

"Yes! I put the bottle in the pantry refrigerator Monday morning and removed it and put Derek's bottle back after he left for the day. It was so easy, but I didn't mean to kill him! I just wanted Derek to suffer a little bit for all the suffering I've gone through since September."

"Poor you," Miranda said.

"It was his own fault. Derek's jealousy did him in. He couldn't bear someone more successful than he was in the department. He was an average professor, an average researcher, and he couldn't deal with the career I'm building."

"Was building. I don't think you'll be making cable news or social media appearances from your prison cell."

Bradley shouted an expletive at Miranda and bounded from the room.

"Don't let him leave!" Susanna started after him.

Miranda grabbed her arm. "He won't get far."

I dashed into the hall. Bradley had his hand on the front door knob. In a second he opened the door and stepped over the threshold.

"What!" He stumbled backwards into the hall.

"Hands up!" Tracey stepped into view from behind the open door. She had her gun drawn but pointed at the floor.

A second officer passed her, spun Bradley around, handcuffed him, and walked him out the door. Tracey followed, reciting Bradley's Miranda rights.

I lingered in the doorway, stunned by what had unfolded and grateful for its conclusion. Now Susanna could truly mourn for her husband and move into the next chapter of her life.

Vicki stood in the middle of her lawn with Eliza and Josie. She gripped both their hands and observed the action. Both girls were quiet and wide-eyed at the presence of the four police cars in the street.

Vicki moved her glance to Susanna's house and spotted me in the doorway. She nodded and mouthed "Well done."

I mouthed my reply. "Team effort."

A soft sob drew my attention away from the outdoor scene. Behind me, Miranda had put her arm around Susanna's shoulder. Susanna pressed her hand against her eyes and choked back another sob. Miranda's eyes glistened; her determined expression had collapsed into one of sorrow.

Derek may've been jealous of Susanna's and Miranda's achievements and tried to thwart their endeavors, but both women cared for him. Now Derek's spouse and his colleague grieved together.

After Susanna, Miranda, and I'd given our statements at the police station, Tracey praised us for our poise during Bradley's *interrogation*. "Best, though, to leave that to the police."

"It gave me a fascinating perspective on interrogation techniques," Miranda said. "I'd love to interview you some time,

Officer Brody. And a few individuals you've questioned. I have my own experience under the hot lights of interrogation, but for the sake of objectivity, I shouldn't be a subject of my own research." A glow lit her cheeks.

The proverbial light bulb has been switched on.

Susanna linked her arm through Miranda's and turned her toward the exit. "Let's go. You're my ride home."

"I'll call you," Miranda said over her shoulder to Tracey.

"Most people don't want anything to do with me after I've questioned them," Tracey quipped.

"Professor Liu isn't most people. You've been Mirandized."

I caught up with the professorial pair; Miranda was my ride home too.

"Should I drop you off at All Things?" Miranda established eye contact with me via her rearview mirror.

"Home, please." I'd called Claire from the station and told her I wouldn't be returning to the shop. I was mentally worn out and didn't want to deal with Claire's and my staff's inquiries about the case's dénouement. I'd save the energy I had left to give Mark a full account.

"You were very impressive," I said to Miranda.

"I channeled my inner soap opera star."

Susanna gave a tired laugh.

"You should audition for the Barton Community Theater's next production."

Miranda's response to my suggestion was a wide smile that filled the rear-view mirror.

We reached my house in a few minutes. Miranda pulled into the driveway and shifted into *Park*, but she left the engine running. "It was a pleasure being a part of your sleuth crew. Brilliant work solving the case, Veronica."

"You gave me the crucial information to solve it."

Susanna slid from the car before I took two steps across the driveway. "Thank you, Veronica."

The short statement and the tight embrace she gave me was all the gratitude I needed. Susanna, however, had more.

"Not only for figuring out who killed Derek but also for everything you've done over the last three weeks. I've appreciated it all." She flashed a look of wonder. "Thank goodness I asked you to help pack Derek's books!"

"I'm always available for a hamburger at the Hearth whenever you need a break from writing your bestselling book with Eric."

"The first signed copy is yours."

Chapter Thirty-Eight

Life had returned to normal by the following Tuesday. Over the intervening four days, I'd told my tale of how I figured out Bradley was Derek's killer several times. I'd received a call from Ashley offering another apology for the aggravation she'd caused and inviting me to lunch to make amends. I accepted both the apology and lunch date.

I also spoke with Vicki, who'd stopped by the boutique to thank me for the advice I'd given her. "I've thought about it and have decided to take the videos off my social media. They're not helping anyone."

"Fantastic decision," I said and gave her a hug.

The Memorial Day holiday weekend, capped off with Monday's parade, had helped Barton residents, including me, put the murder case out of our thoughts.

Carol and I sat on a bench outside the bakery and enjoyed slices of crumb cake and coffee.

"I can never again tell my Freudian slip joke," I said. "It will always remind me of Derek. What a psycho-drama this has been."

"I'm calling a moratorium on the psychology puns and lingo." Carol gave me an amused side-eye, and popped a small piece of crumb cake into her mouth.

"Good morning, Veronica!" The chirpy greeting came from Miranda. She was halfway across Orchard Street and headed for our bench. She introduced herself to Carol and babbled for a half-minute about how it would be fascinating to do a study on the best friends of famous people. "It would be an interesting view on self-esteem and the psychological effects of being fame-adjacent."

Carol shot me another sideways glance, one much less humored than the first. I knew the moratorium would be extended to psychobabble the moment Miranda was out of earshot.

"A future paper. I have to finish my current research, which has barely begun. Veronica, when can we meet again for another interview?" Miranda whipped out her cell and tapped on its screen. "How's tomorrow at two?"

"Sure." *Do I have a choice?*

"Wonderful." More screen tapping. "We should make this a weekly date."

"How many times do you have to interview me?" Panic surged through me.

"Until I've plumbed the depths of your psyche."

For my own sanity, I interpreted Miranda's smile to mean she was teasing me.

I hope, I hope, I hope she's pulling my leg.

"And I had the most wonderful idea last night! I want you to meet with all my classes and tell them how you created your character. They'll be fascinated. And I'm thinking of adding a new course to my schedule. A study of a select number of characters from film and television. My students and I will examine their psychological makeup. The heroes and villains. What makes them tick and why they've fascinated audiences." Miranda wiggled her fingers in goodbye. "Until tomorrow!" She darted into the bakery.

"She's a whirlwind." Carol wadded her napkin and stuffed it into her empty coffee cup.

"That's an understatement," I said.

"She better not have designs on becoming your best friend forever."

I stretched my arm around Carol and pulled her close. "I'll go berserk if she does."

"Then she'll want to meet with you twice a week." Carol tapped my knee. "And write a whole book on you."

I yawned with comic exaggeration. "Boring."

Carol got up and dumped her cup in a nearby trash can. I stayed on the bench, recovering my wits from Miranda's frenzied conversation.

"I've been Mirandized," I murmured.

Carol laughed and, after a few seconds, I did too.

"It's good to have a psychologist for a friend," I said. "More free therapy. I just hope I don't make any Freudian slips."

Jeanne Quigley is the author of the Veronica Walsh Mysteries and the Robyn Cavanagh Mysteries. Unlike her fictional sleuths, she has never been a soap opera star, accountant, or professional photographer, but she has worked in the music industry, for an educational publisher, and in a county agency. A lifelong New Yorker, Jeanne lives in her native Rockland County.

jeannequigley.wordpress.com
facebook.com/jeannemquigley

Made in the USA
Middletown, DE
30 October 2023

41625336R00144